Dear parents, caregivers, and educators:

If you want to get your child excited about reading, you've come to the right place! Ready-to-Read *GRAPHICS* is the perfect launchpad for emerging graphic novel readers.

All Ready-to-Read *GRAPHICS* books include the following:

- ★ **A how-to guide to reading graphic novels for first-time readers**

- ★ **Easy-to-follow panels to support reading comprehension**

- ★ **Accessible vocabulary to build your child's reading confidence**

- ★ **Compelling stories that star your child's favorite characters**

- ★ **Fresh, engaging illustrations that provide context and promote visual literacy**

Wherever your child may be on their reading journey, Ready-to-Read *GRAPHICS* will make them giggle, gasp, and want to keep reading more.

Blast off on this starry adventure . . . a universe of graphic novel reading awaits!

& BOONE

The BIG Cheese

written and illustrated by
Janee Trasler

Ready-to-Read **GRAPHICS**

SIMON SPOTLIGHT

An imprint of Simon & Schuster Children's Publishing Division • New York London Toronto Sydney New Delhi
1230 Avenue of the Americas, New York, New York 10020
This Simon Spotlight edition January 2023 • Copyright © 2023 by Janee Trasler • All rights reserved, including the right of reproduction in whole or in part in any form.
SIMON SPOTLIGHT, READY-TO-READ, and colophon are registered trademarks of Simon & Schuster, Inc. • For information about special discounts for bulk purchases,
please contact Simon & Schuster Special Sales at 1-866-506-1949 or business@simonandschuster.com. • Manufactured in China 0922 SCP
2 4 6 8 10 9 7 5 3 1
This book has been cataloged with the Library of Congress.
ISBN 978-1-6659-1452-9 (hc)
ISBN 978-1-6659-1451-2 (pbk)
ISBN 978-1-6659-1453-6 (ebook)

How to Read This Book

This is Figgy. He's here to give you some tips on reading this book.

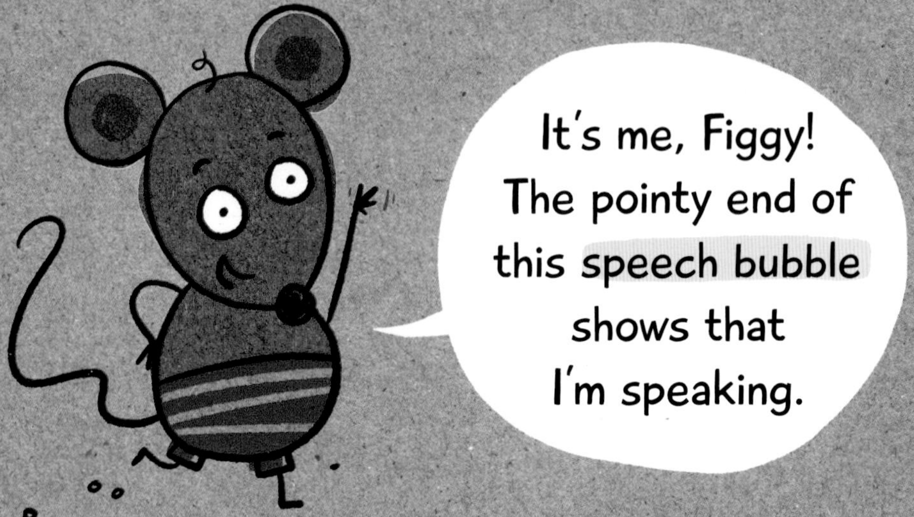
It's me, Figgy! The pointy end of this speech bubble shows that I'm speaking.

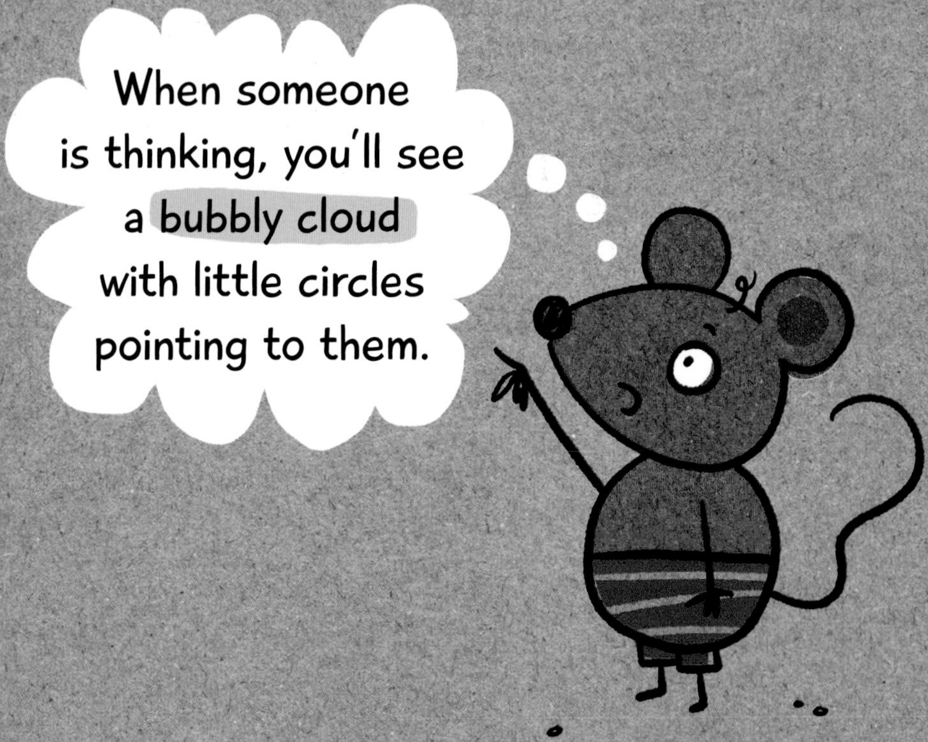
When someone is thinking, you'll see a bubbly cloud with little circles pointing to them.

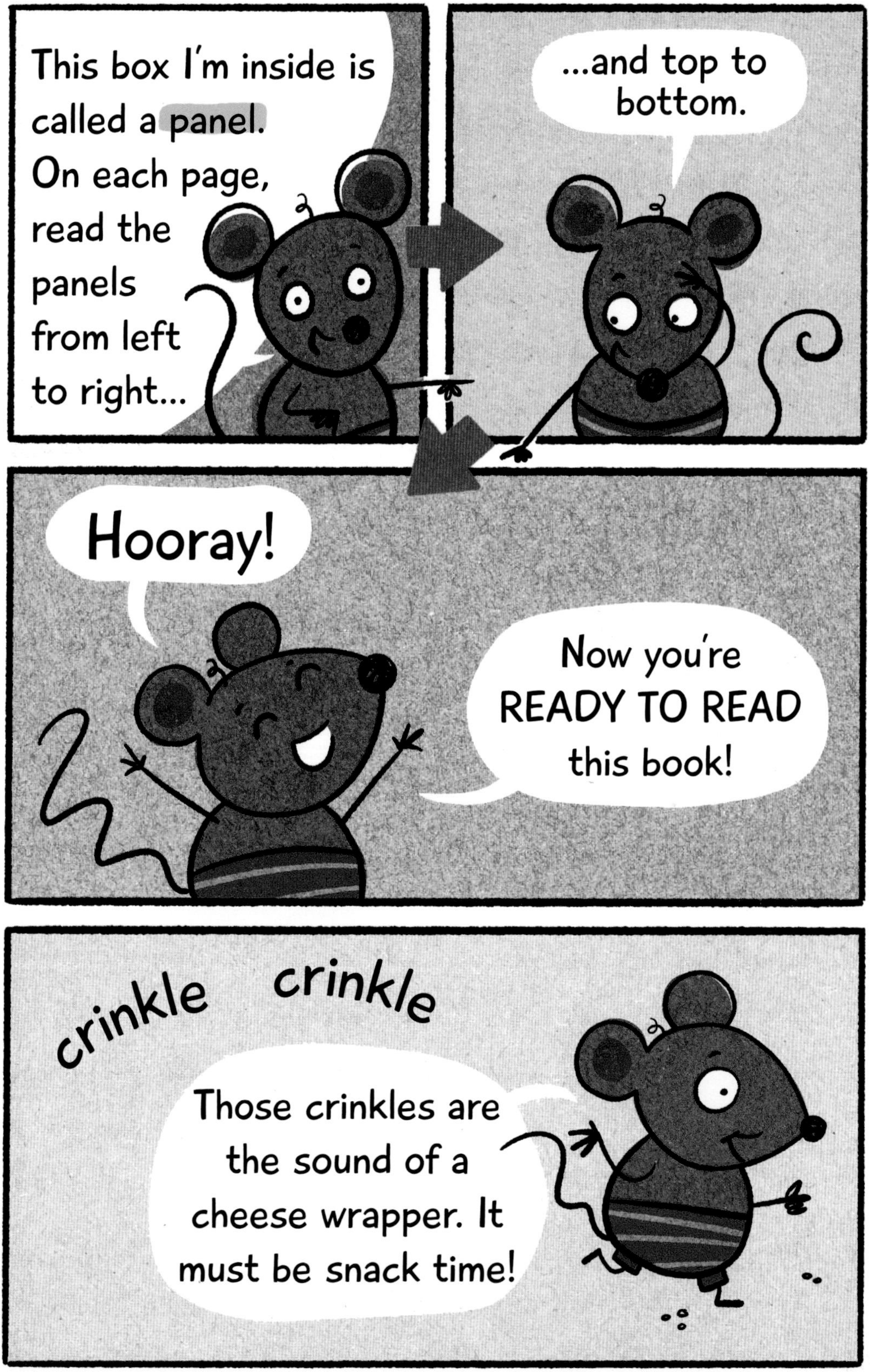
This box I'm inside is called a panel. On each page, read the panels from left to right...
...and top to bottom.
Hooray!
Now you're READY TO READ this book!
crinkle crinkle
Those crinkles are the sound of a cheese wrapper. It must be snack time!

CONTENTS

How To Read This Book   2

Chapter 1: Cheese, Please   5

Chapter 2: The Big Cheese   25

Chapter 3: A Cheesy Idea   55

Chapter 1
Cheese, Please

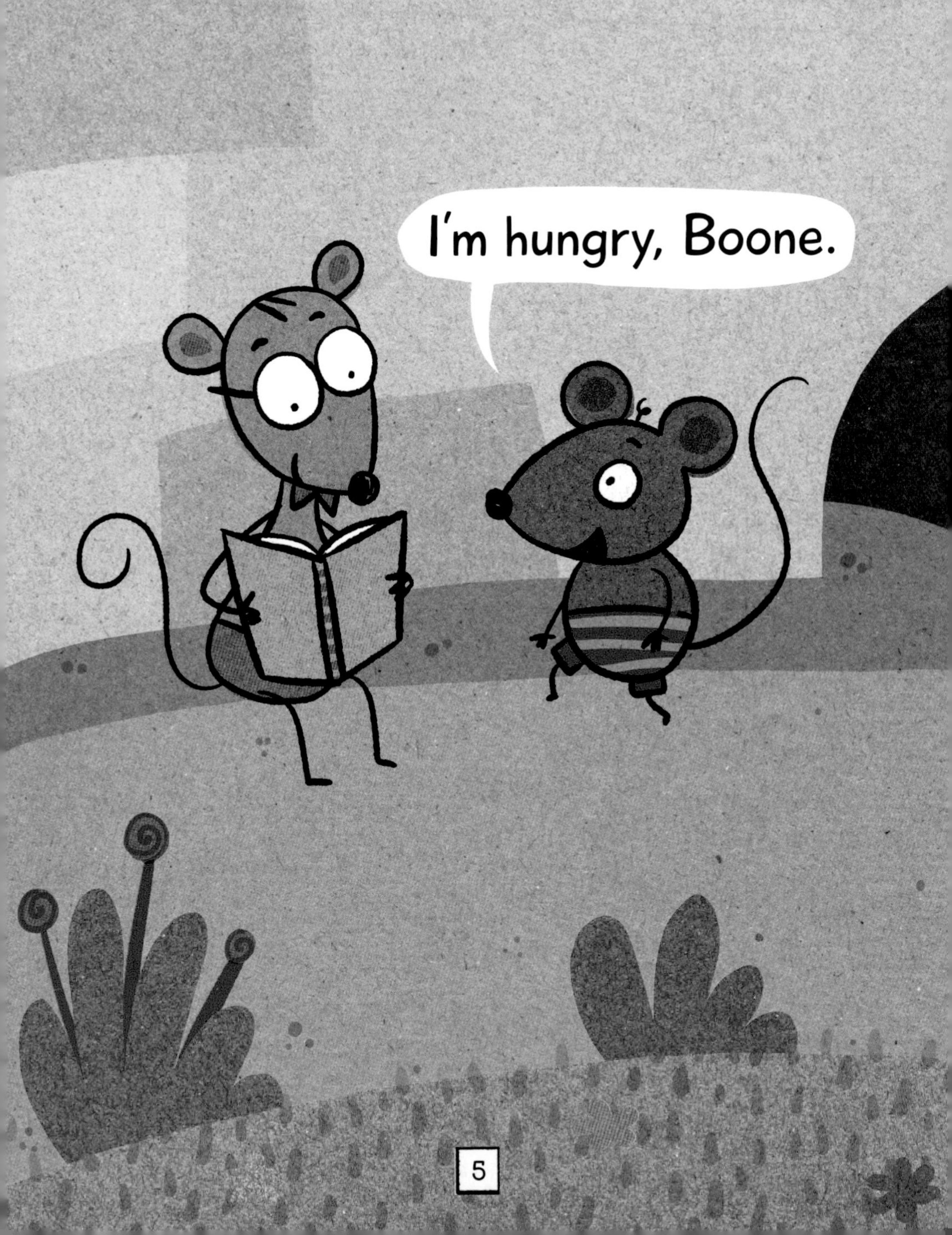
I'm hungry, Boone.

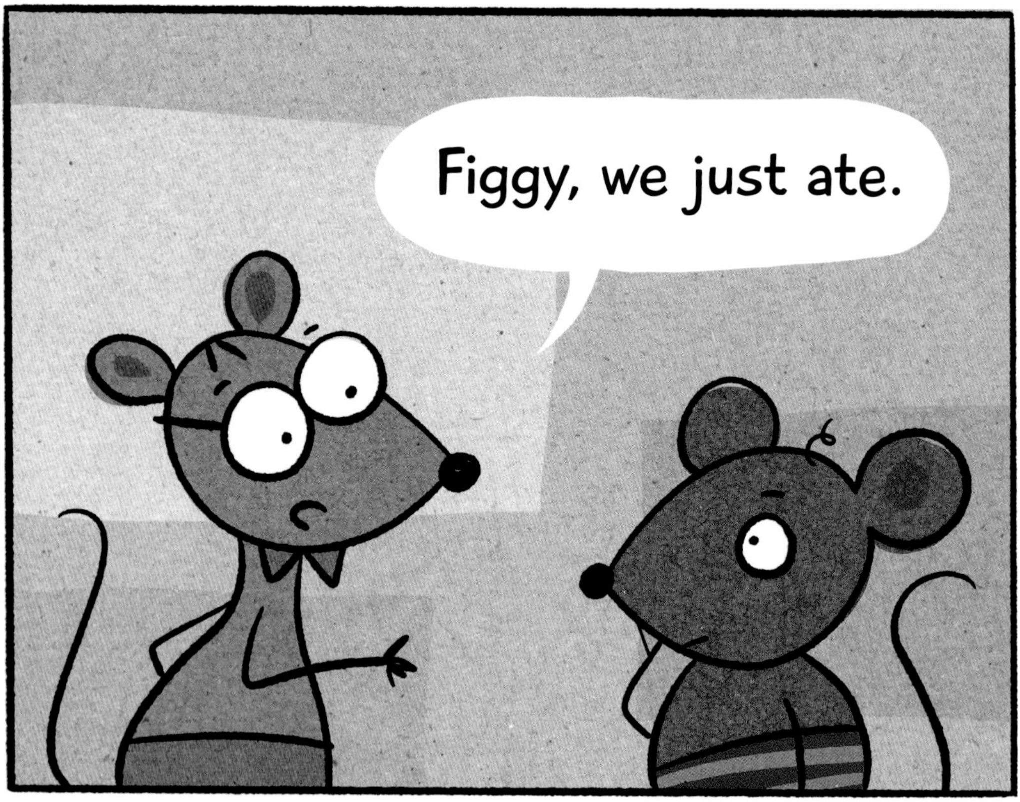
Figgy, we just ate.

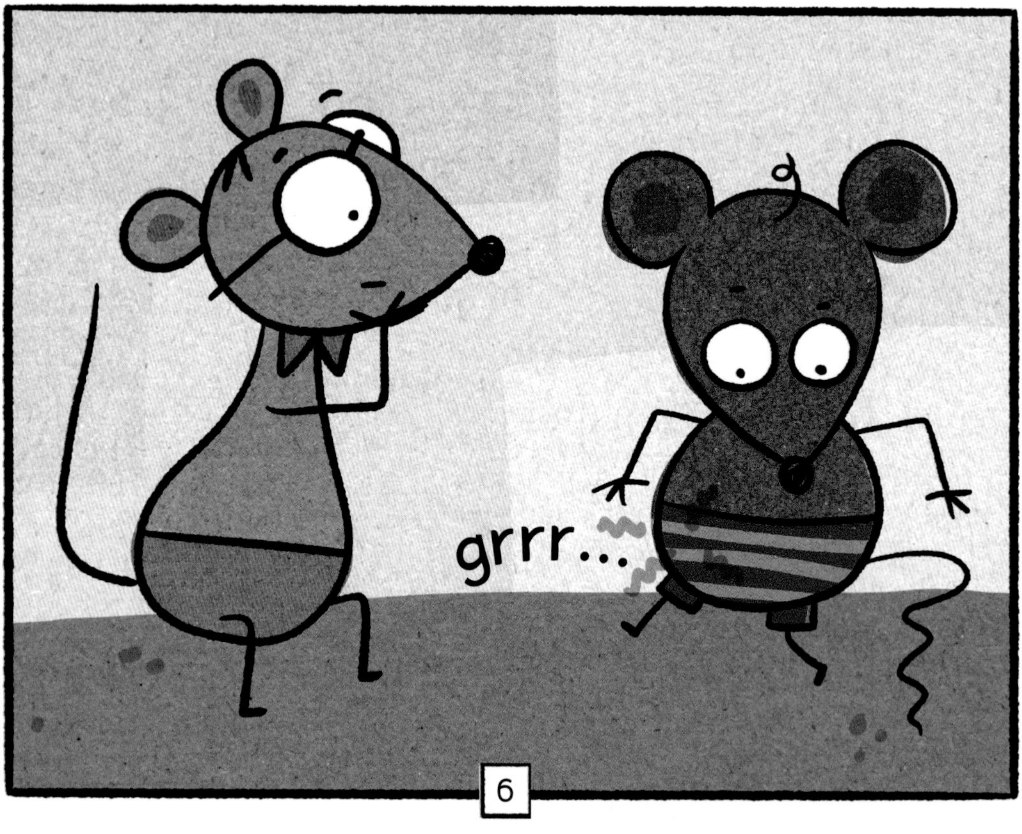
grrr...

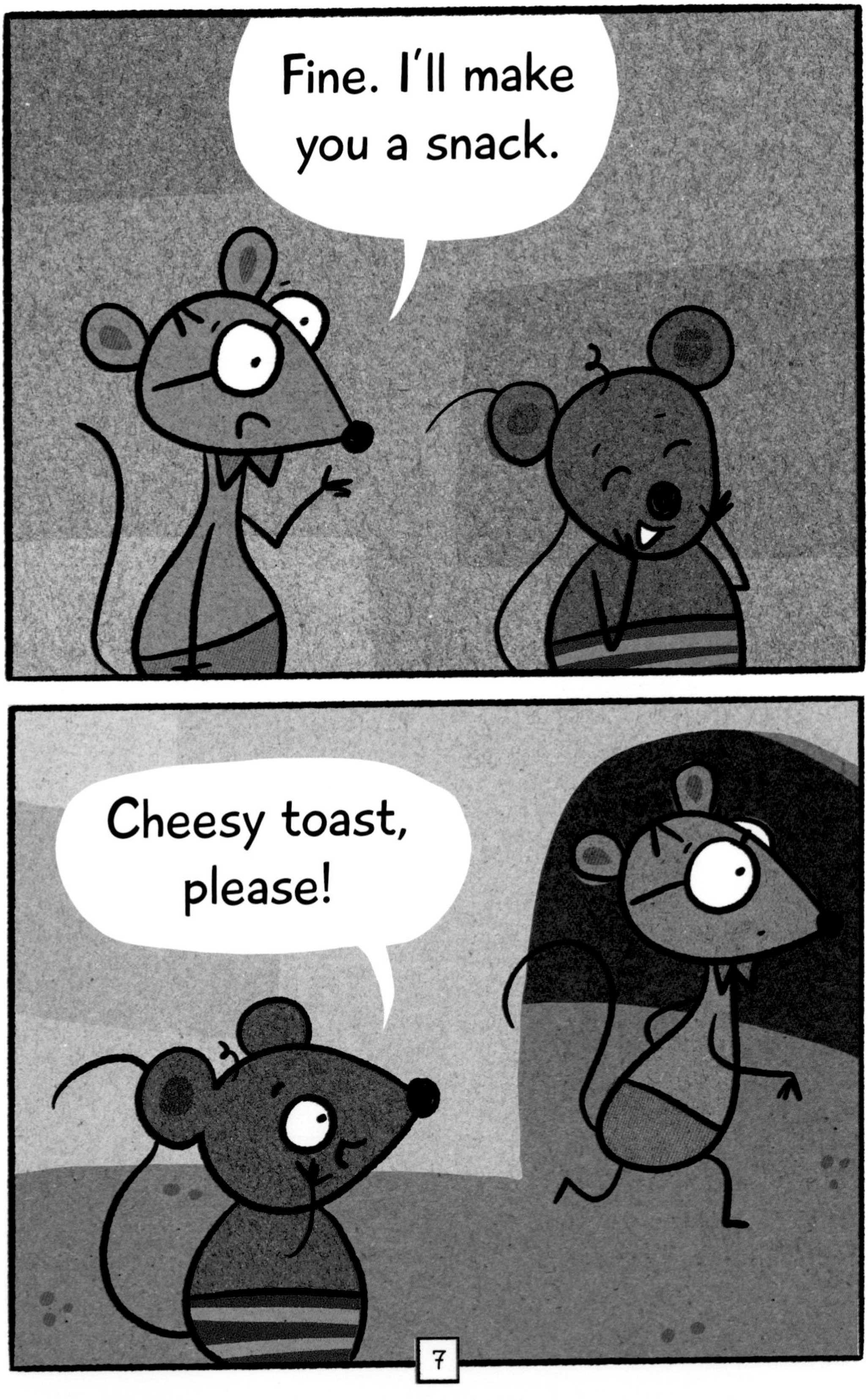
Fine. I'll make you a snack.
Cheesy toast, please!

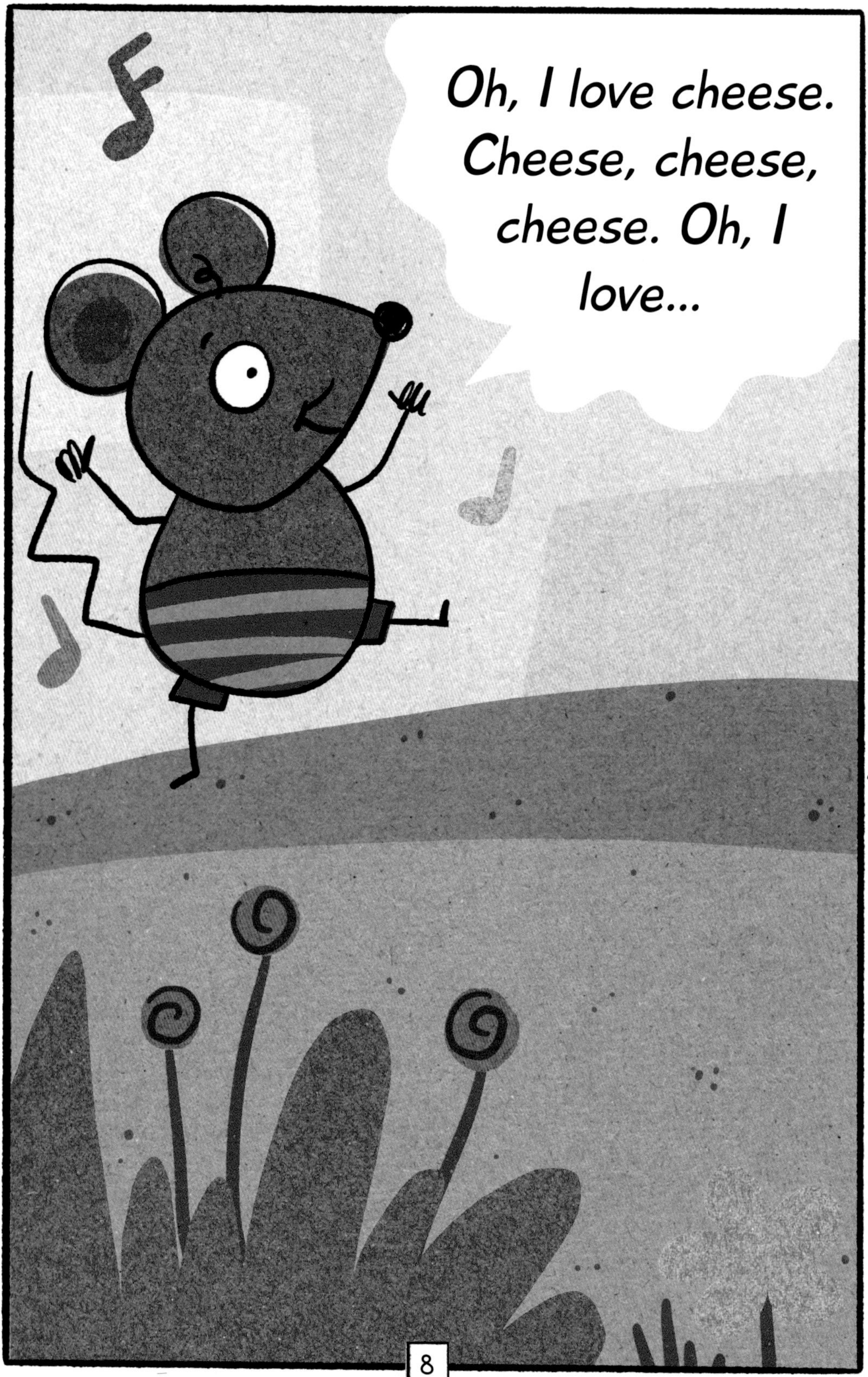
Oh, I love cheese. Cheese, cheese, cheese. Oh, I love...

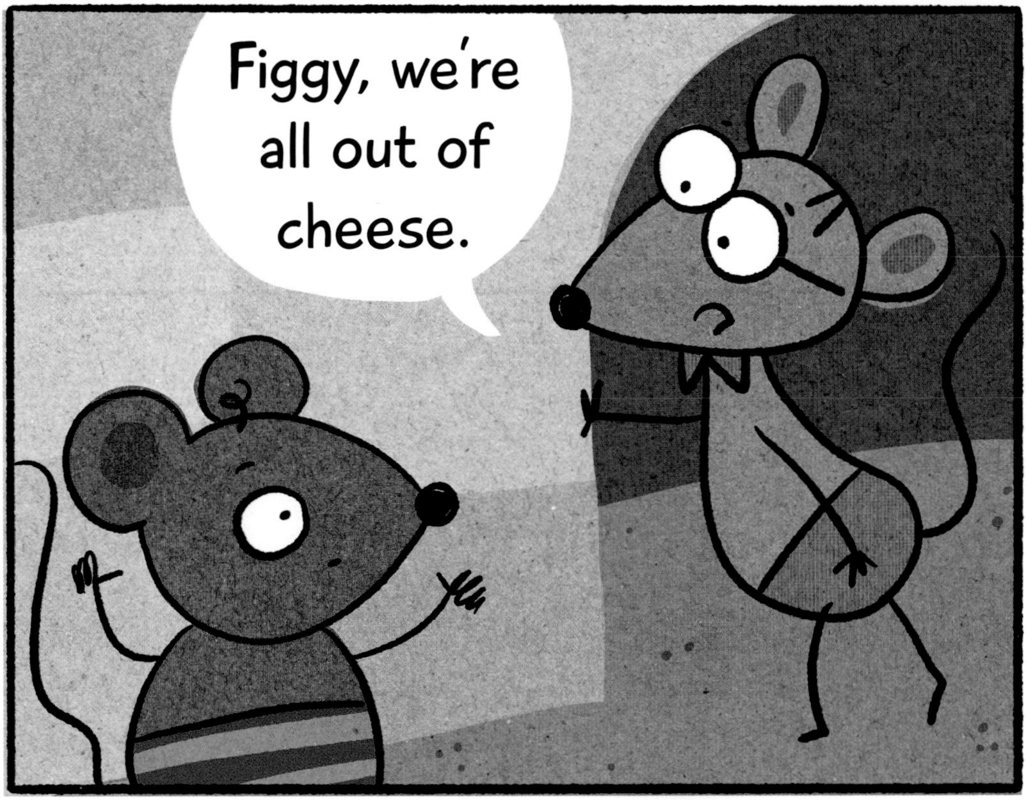
Figgy, we're all out of cheese.

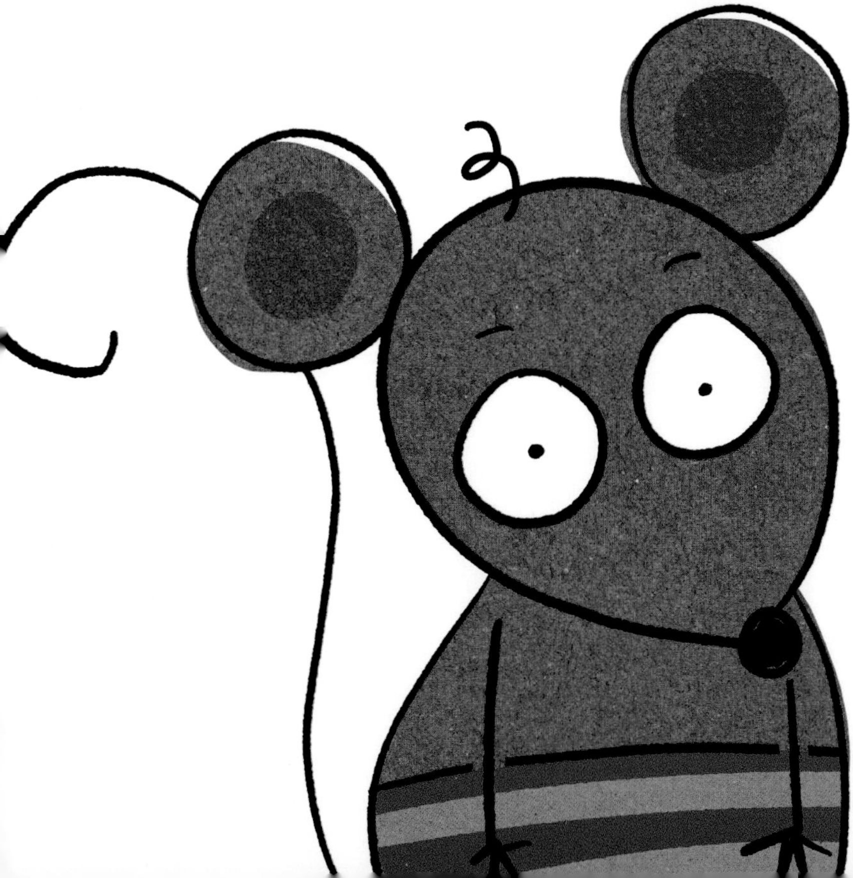

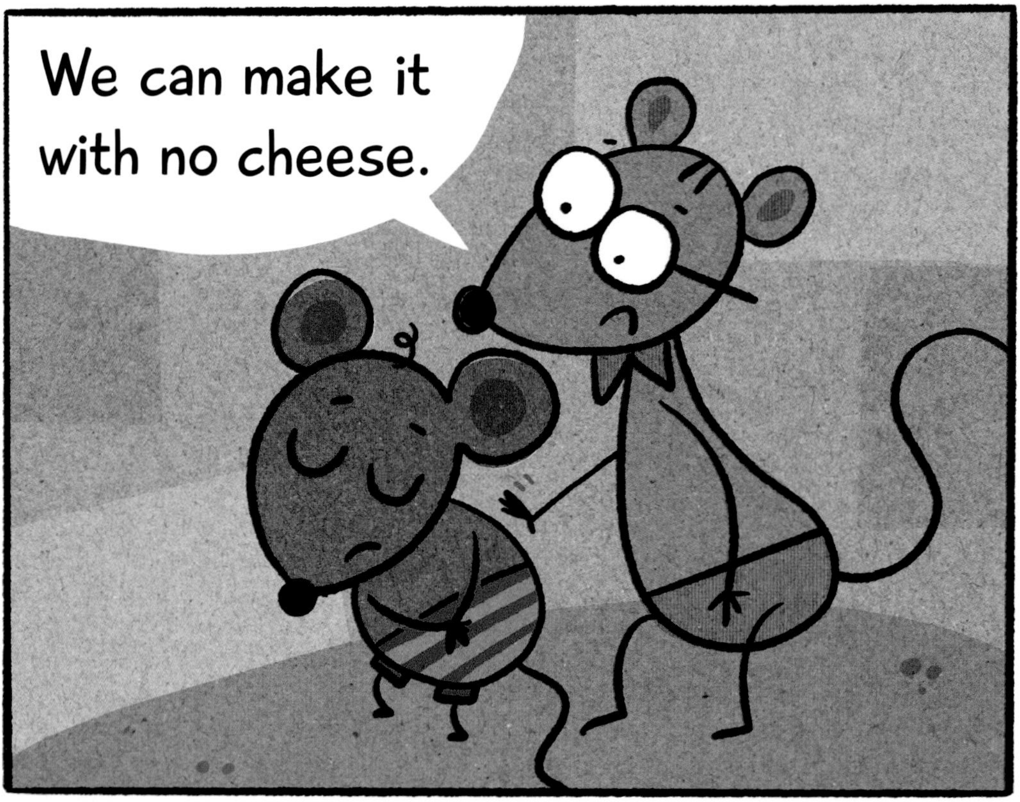
We can make it with no cheese.

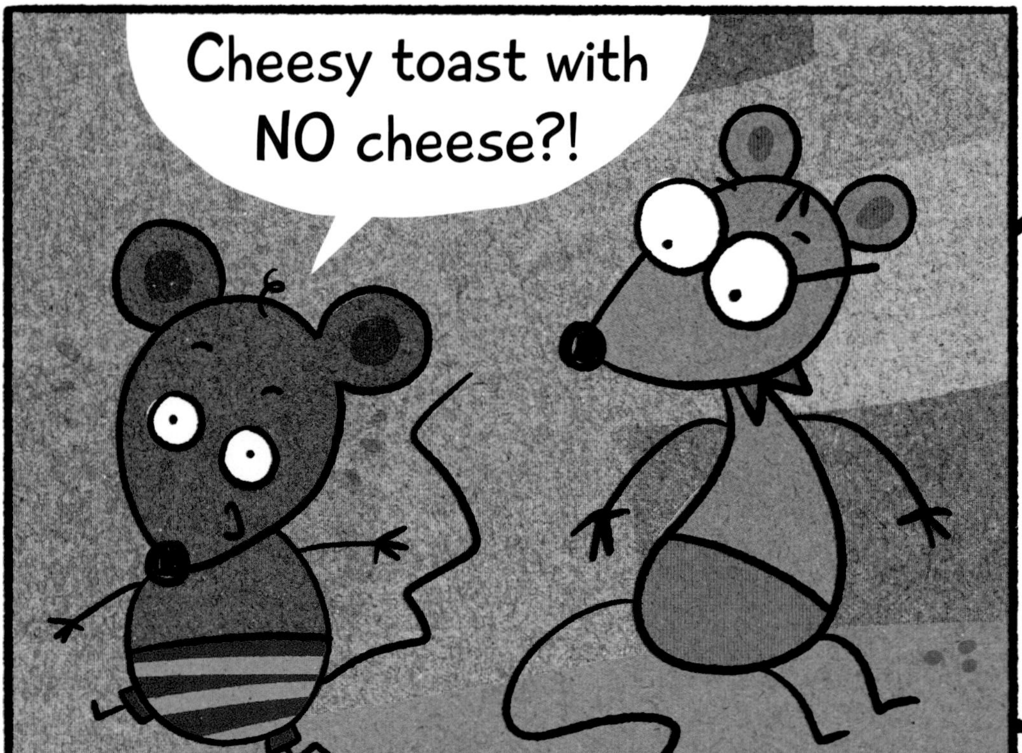
Cheesy toast with NO cheese?!

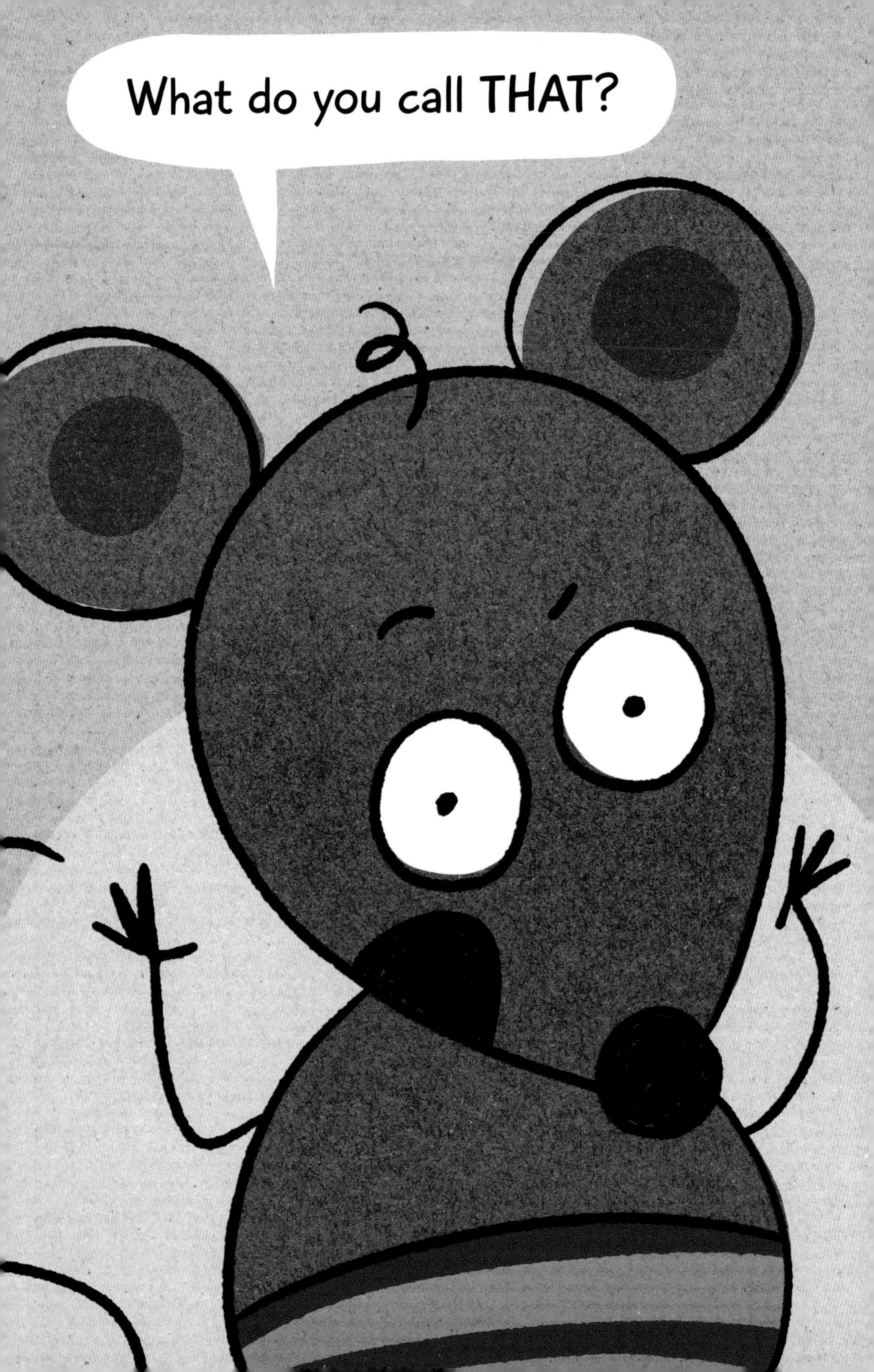
What do you call THAT?

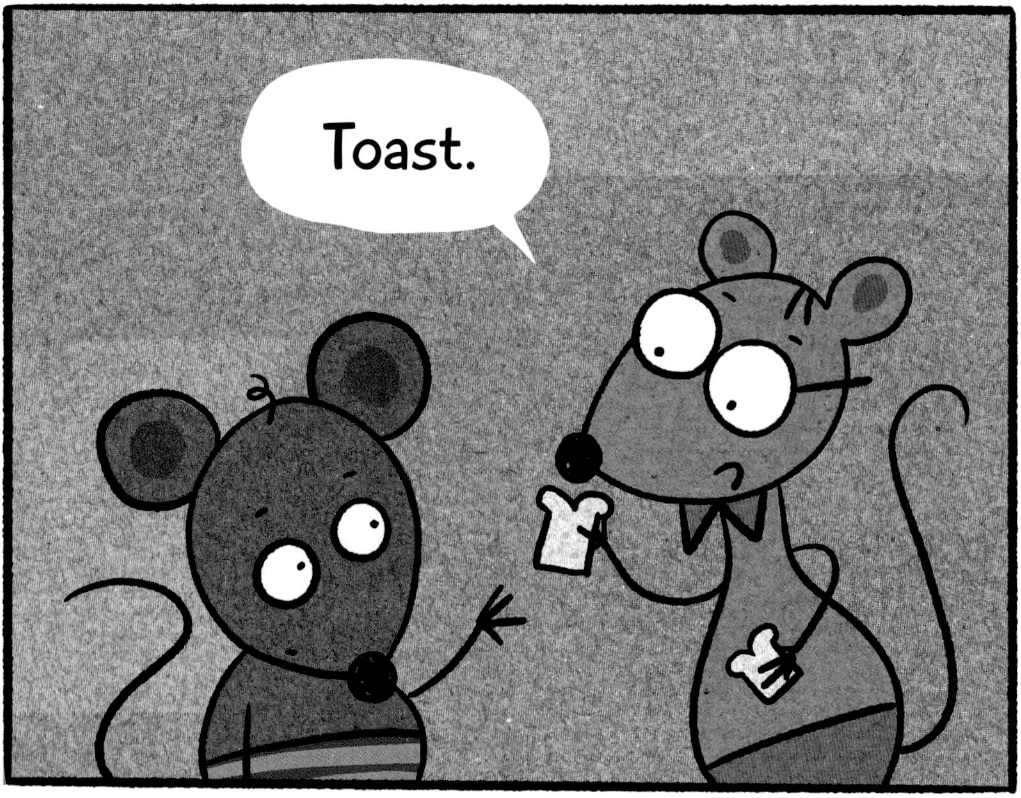
Toast.

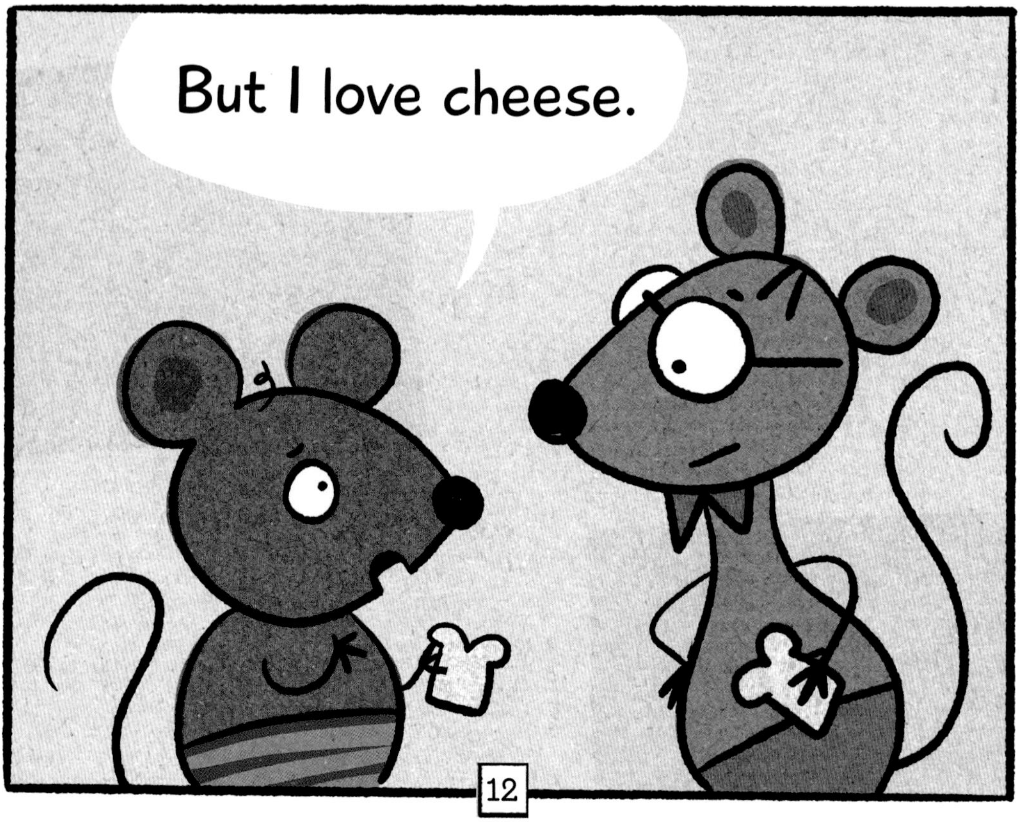
But I love cheese.

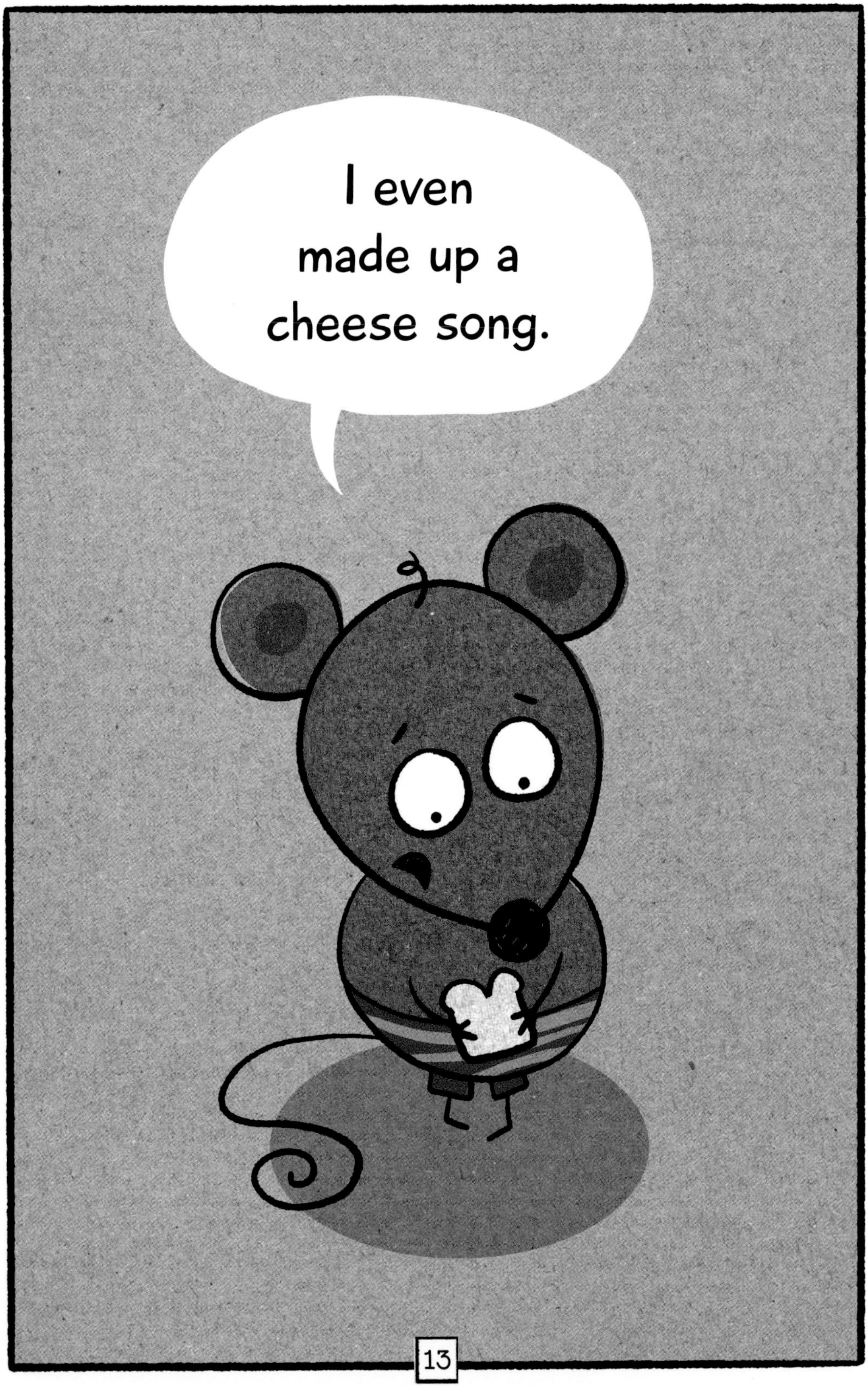
I even made up a cheese song.

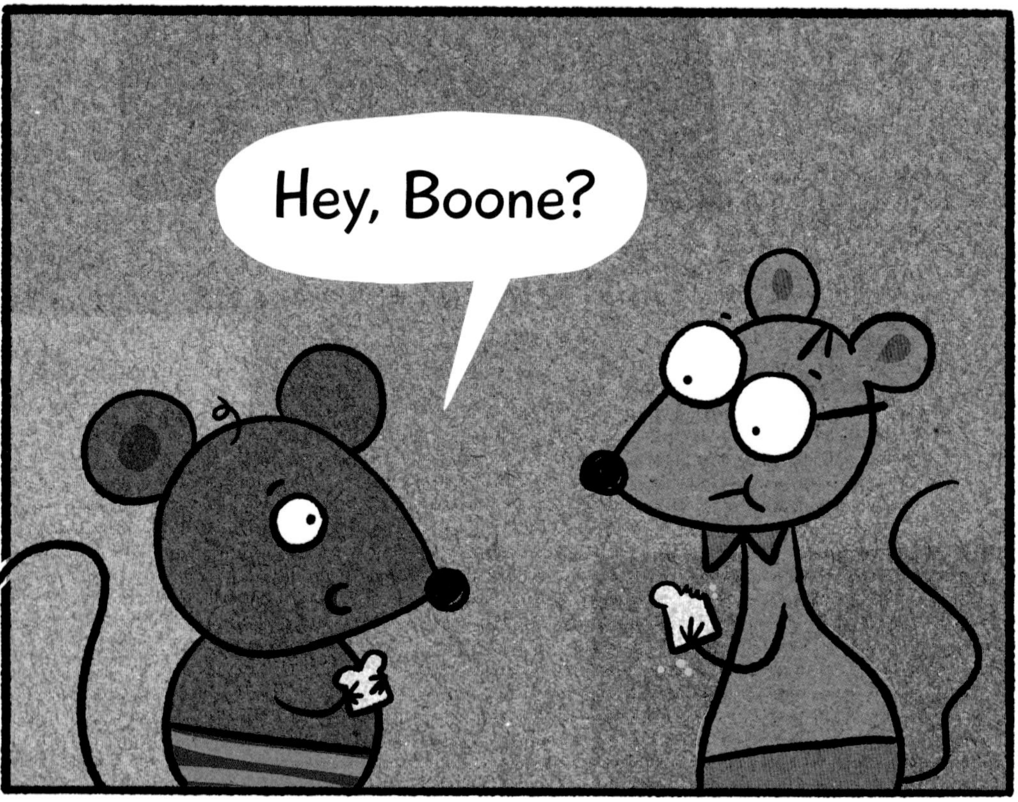
Hey, Boone?

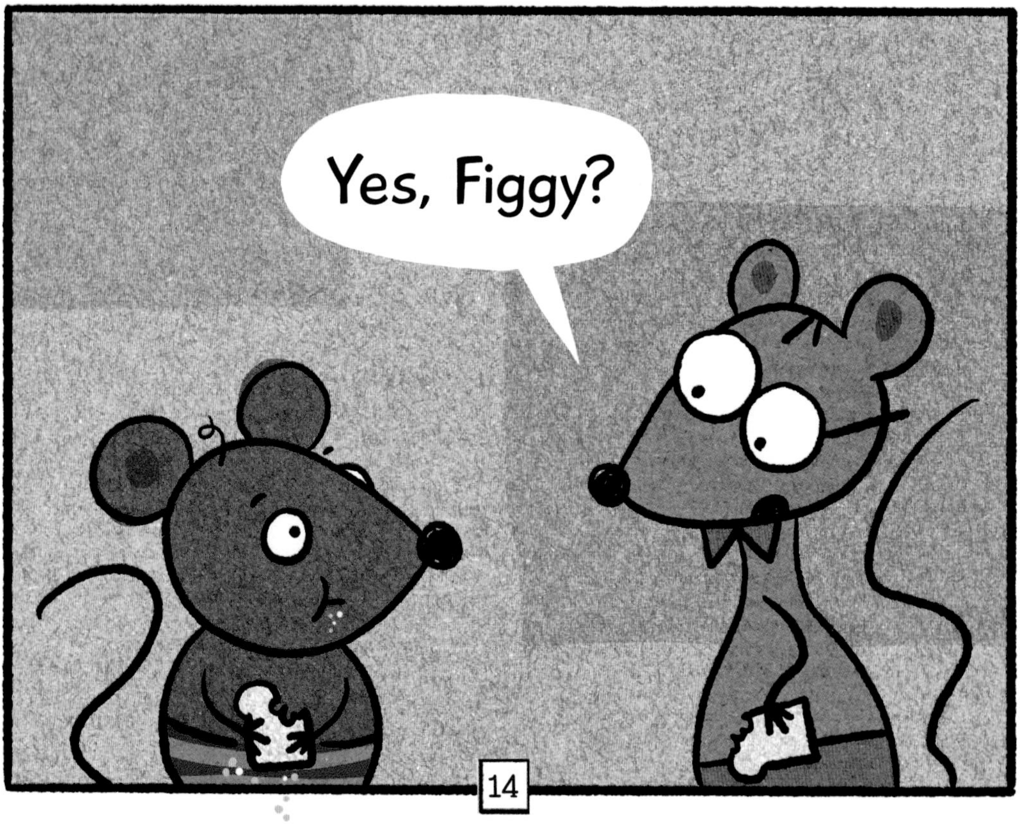
Yes, Figgy?

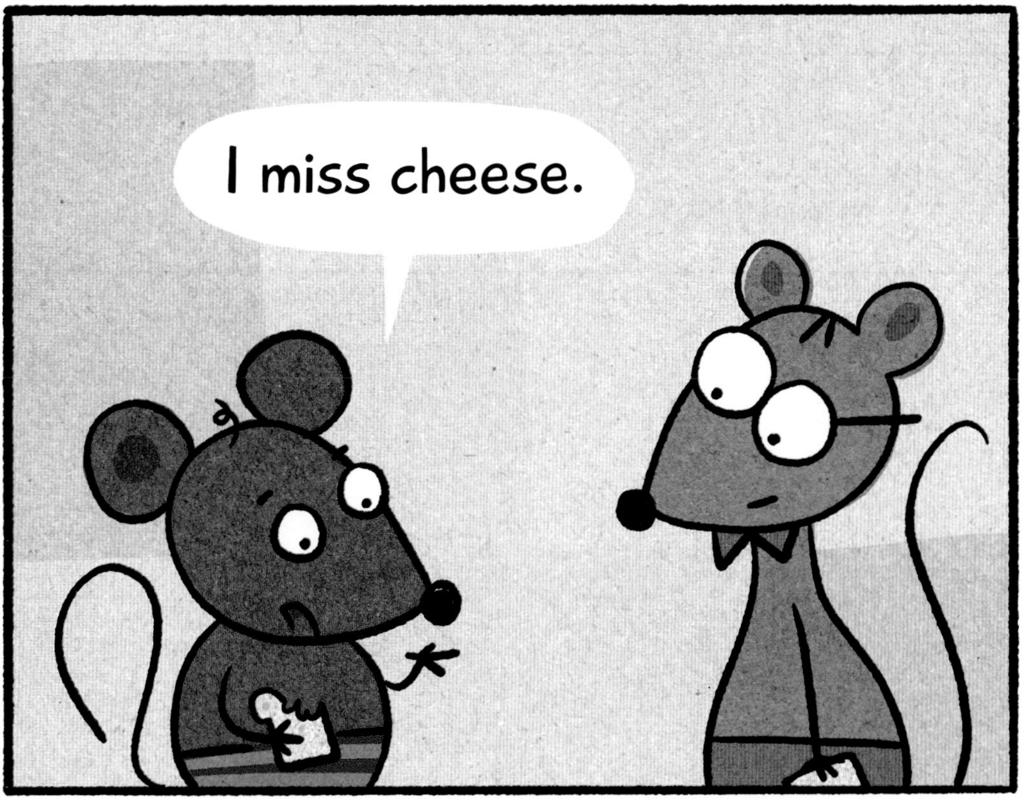
I miss cheese.

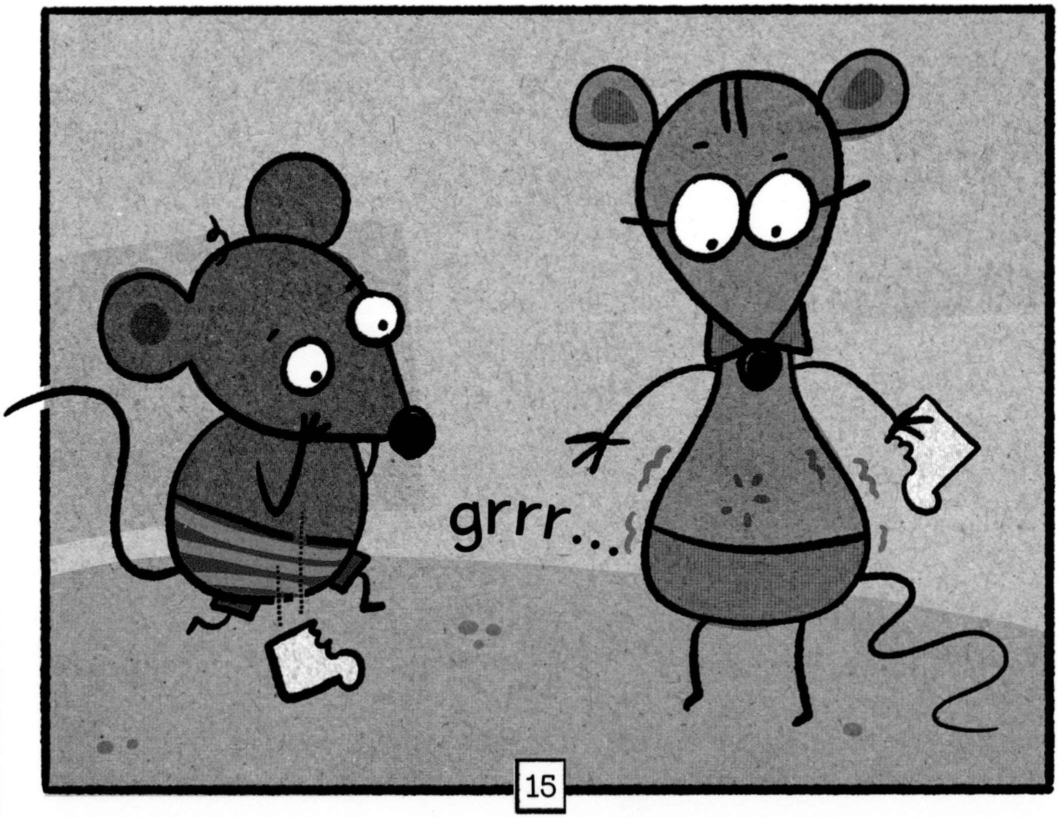
grrr...

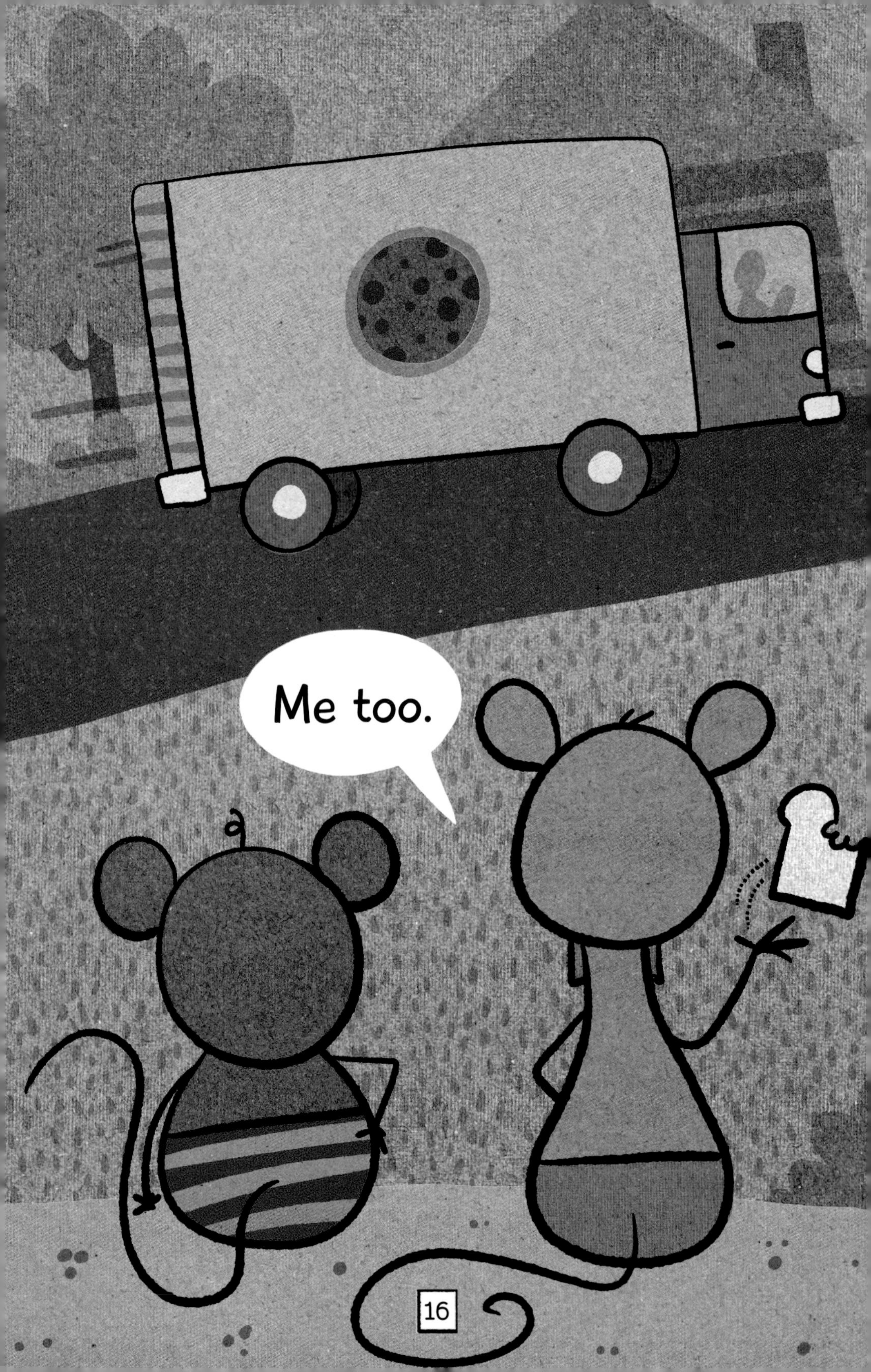
Me too.

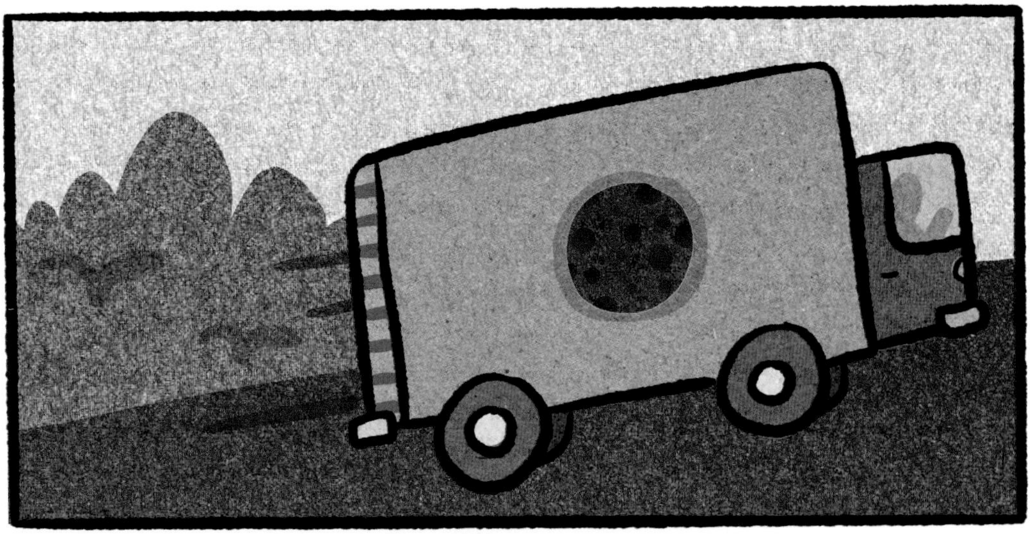

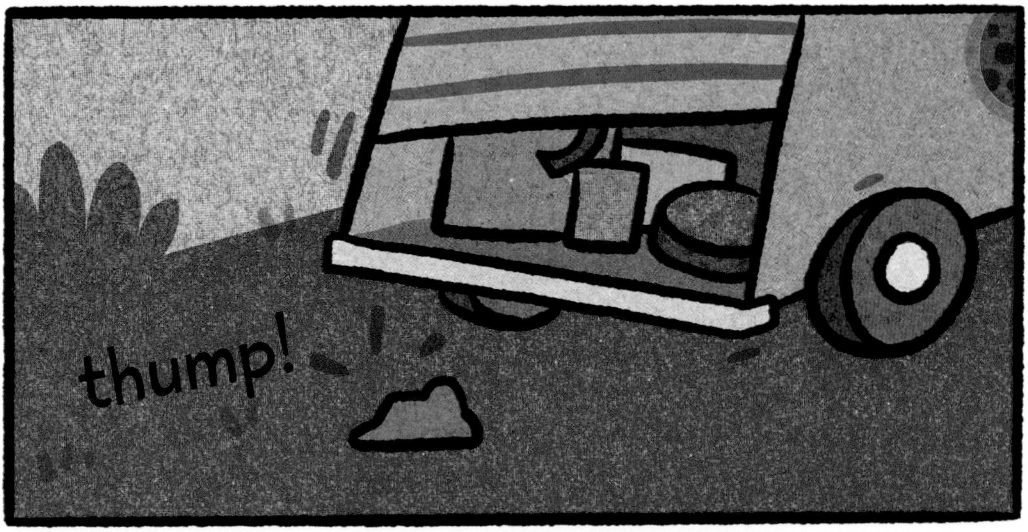
thump!

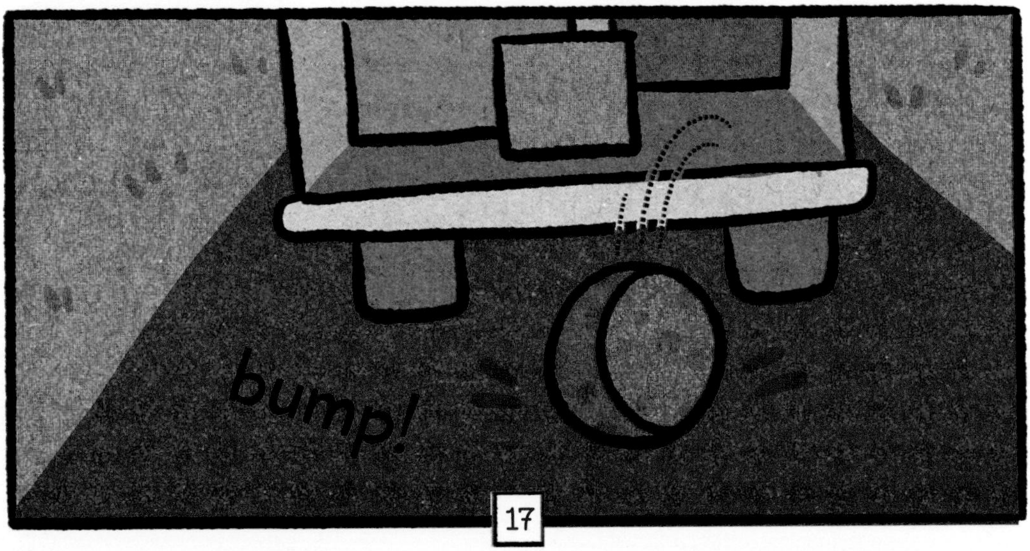
bump!

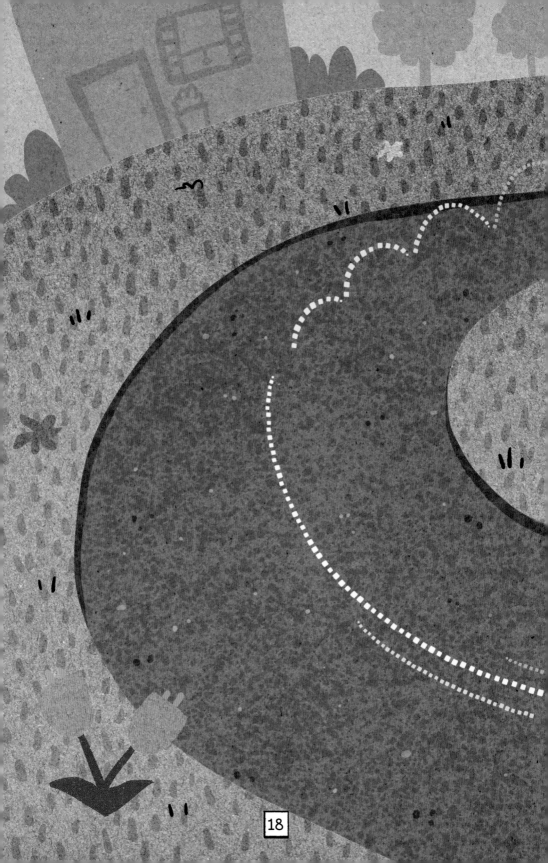

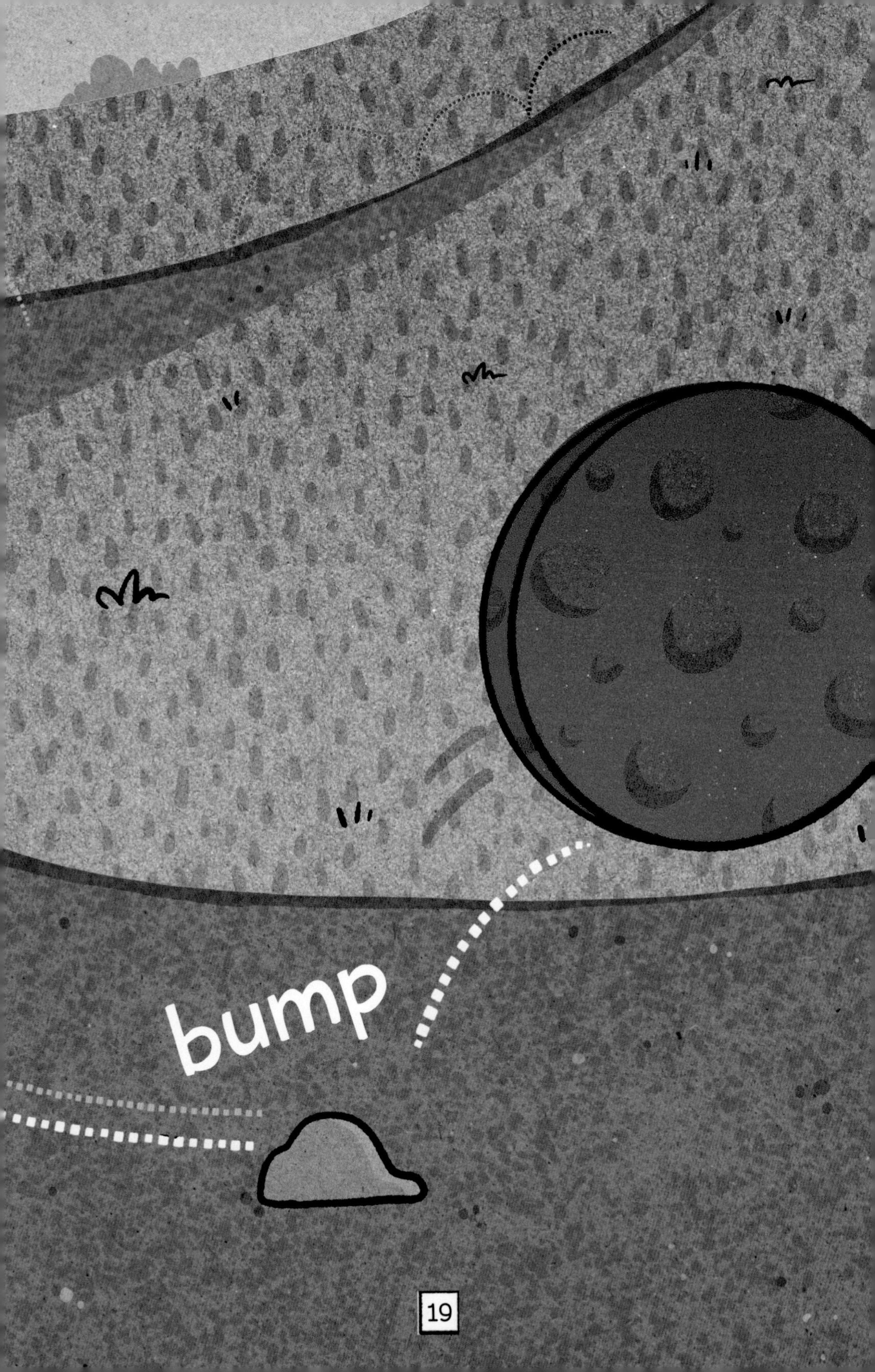
bump

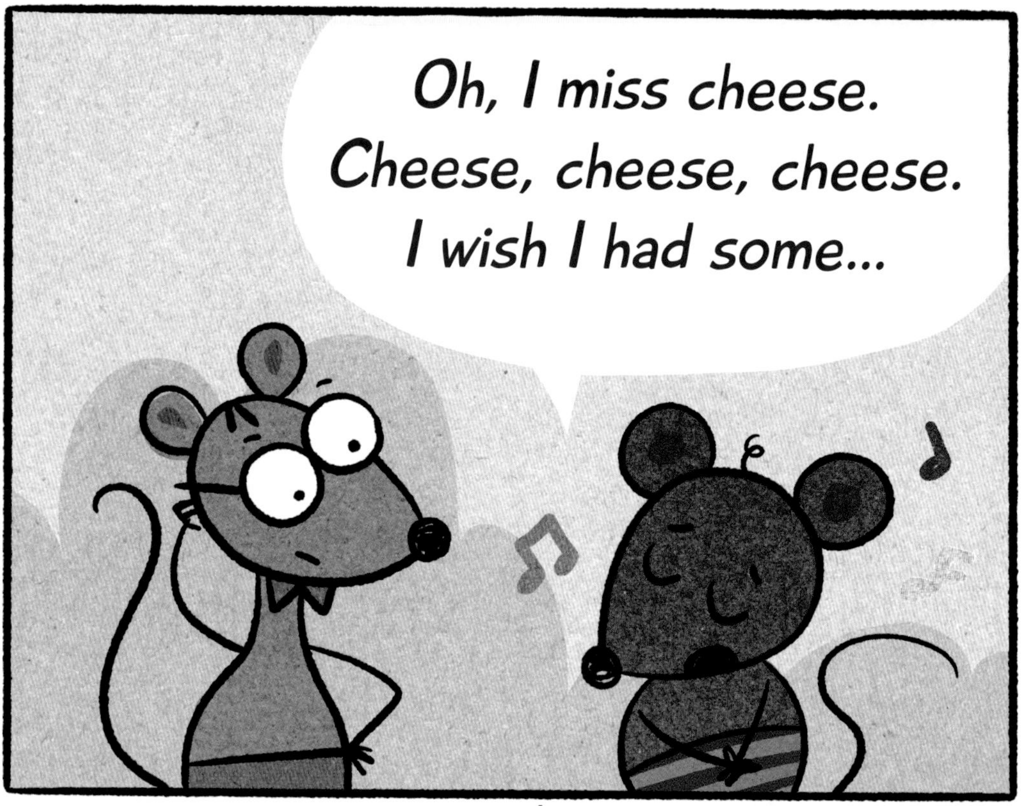
Oh, I miss cheese.
Cheese, cheese, cheese.
I wish I had some...

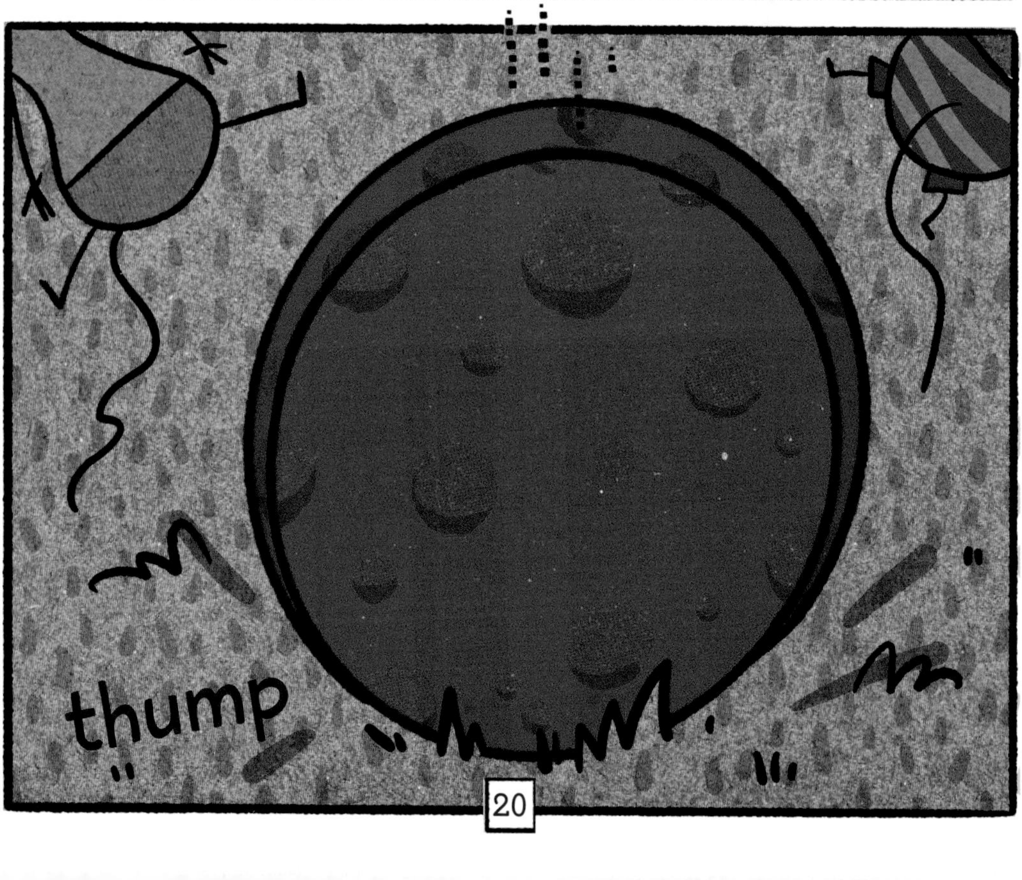
thump

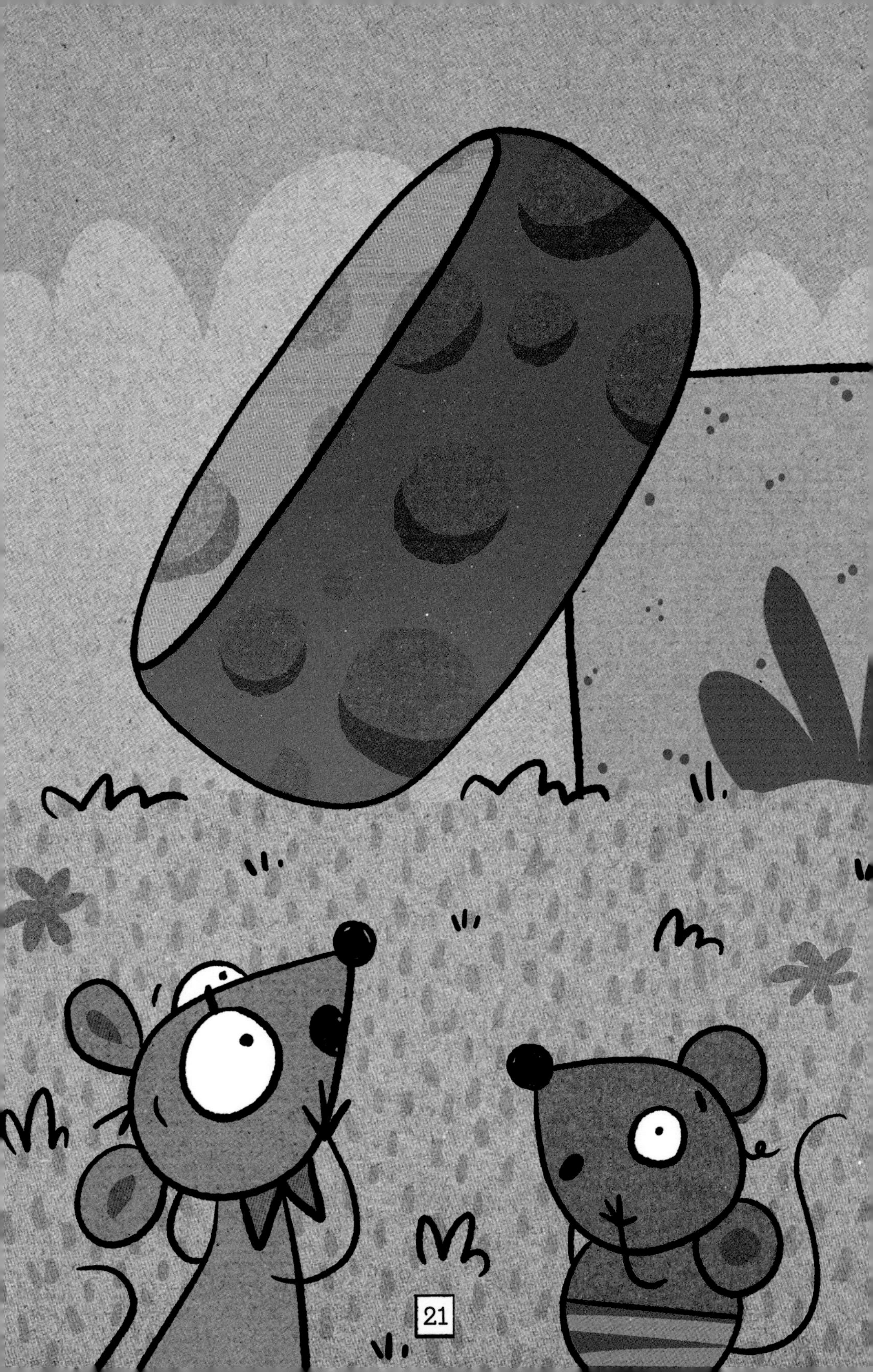

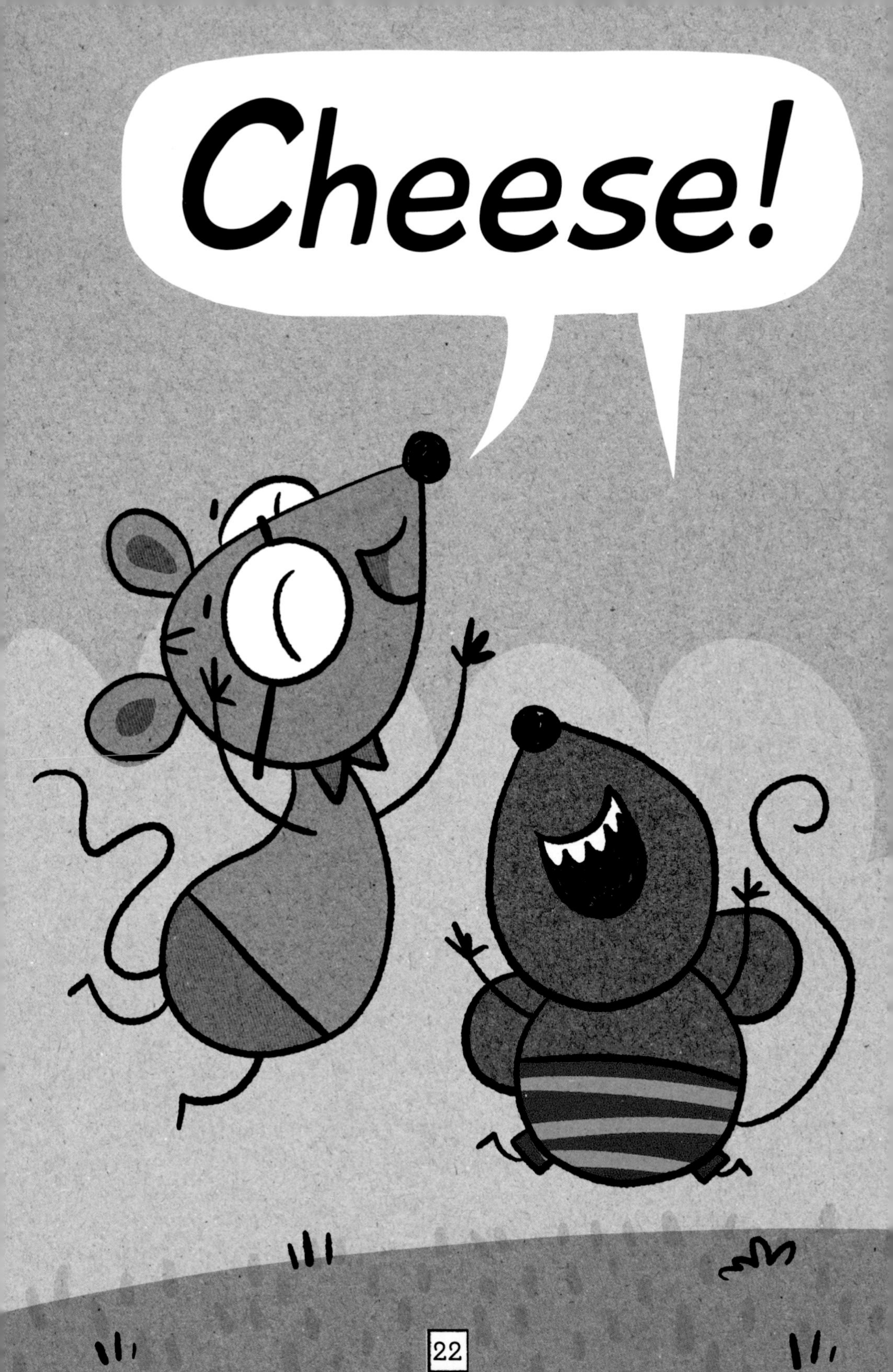
Cheese!

Boone's Guide
to Cheese

 1. Soft cheese:
Spread on
crackers or bread.

 2. Hard cheese:
Use in a sandwich
or on toast.

 3. Scary cheese:
Run! Run away!

Figgy's Guide to Cheese

1. Eat it.

2. Eat it all.

Chapter 2
The Big Cheese

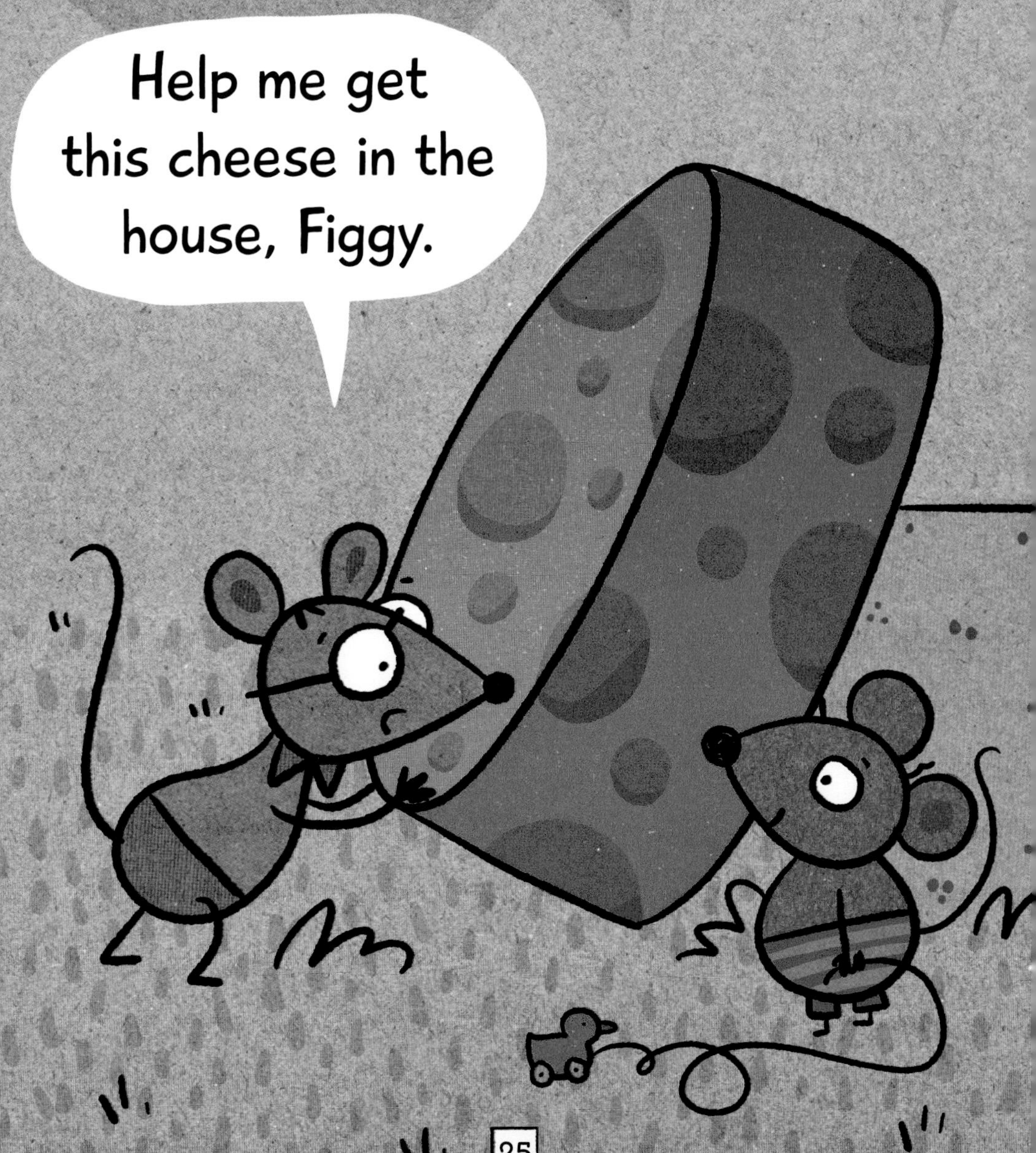
Help me get this cheese in the house, Figgy.

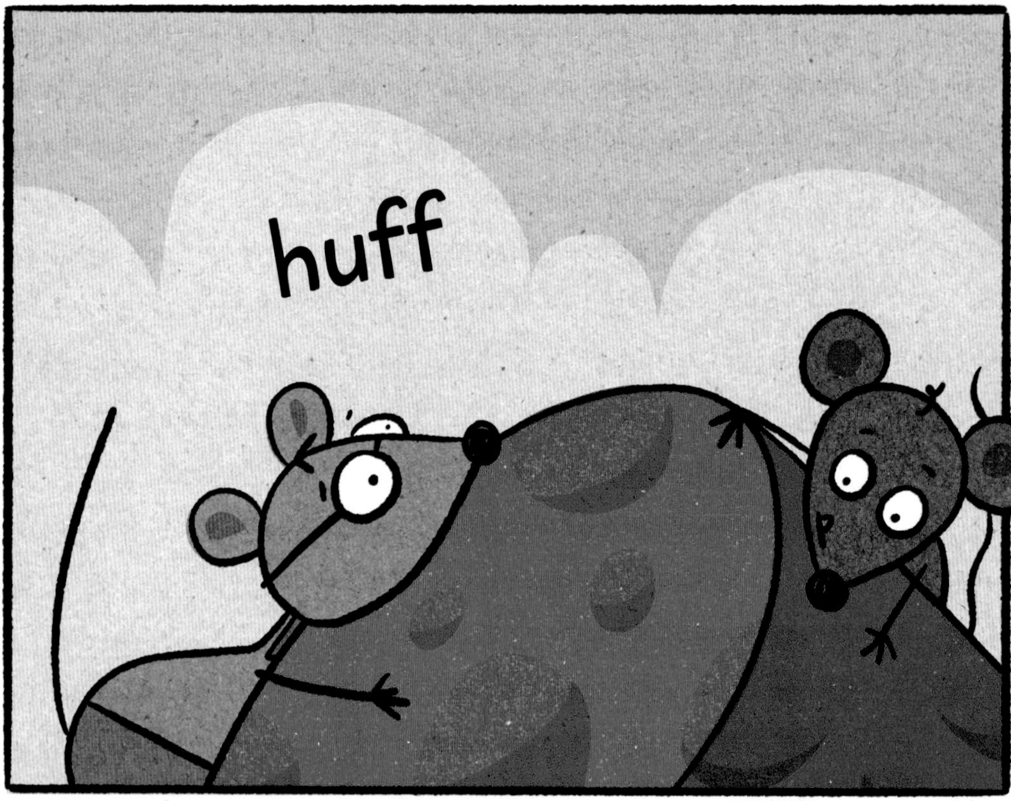
huff

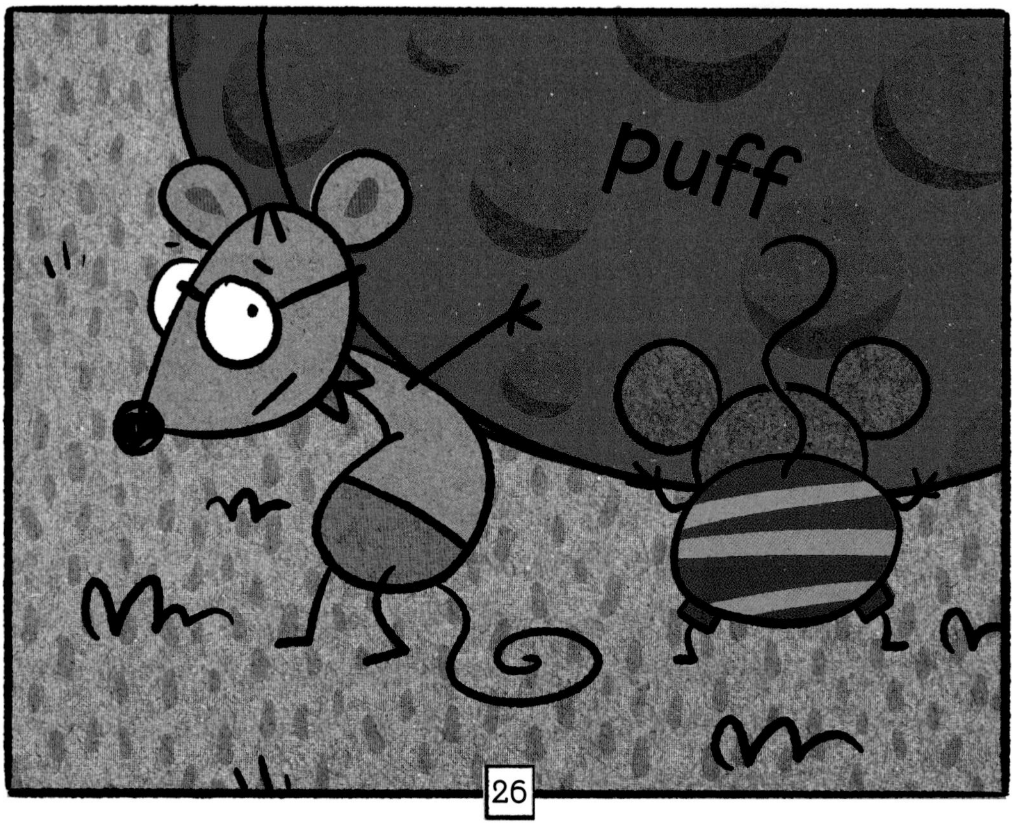
puff

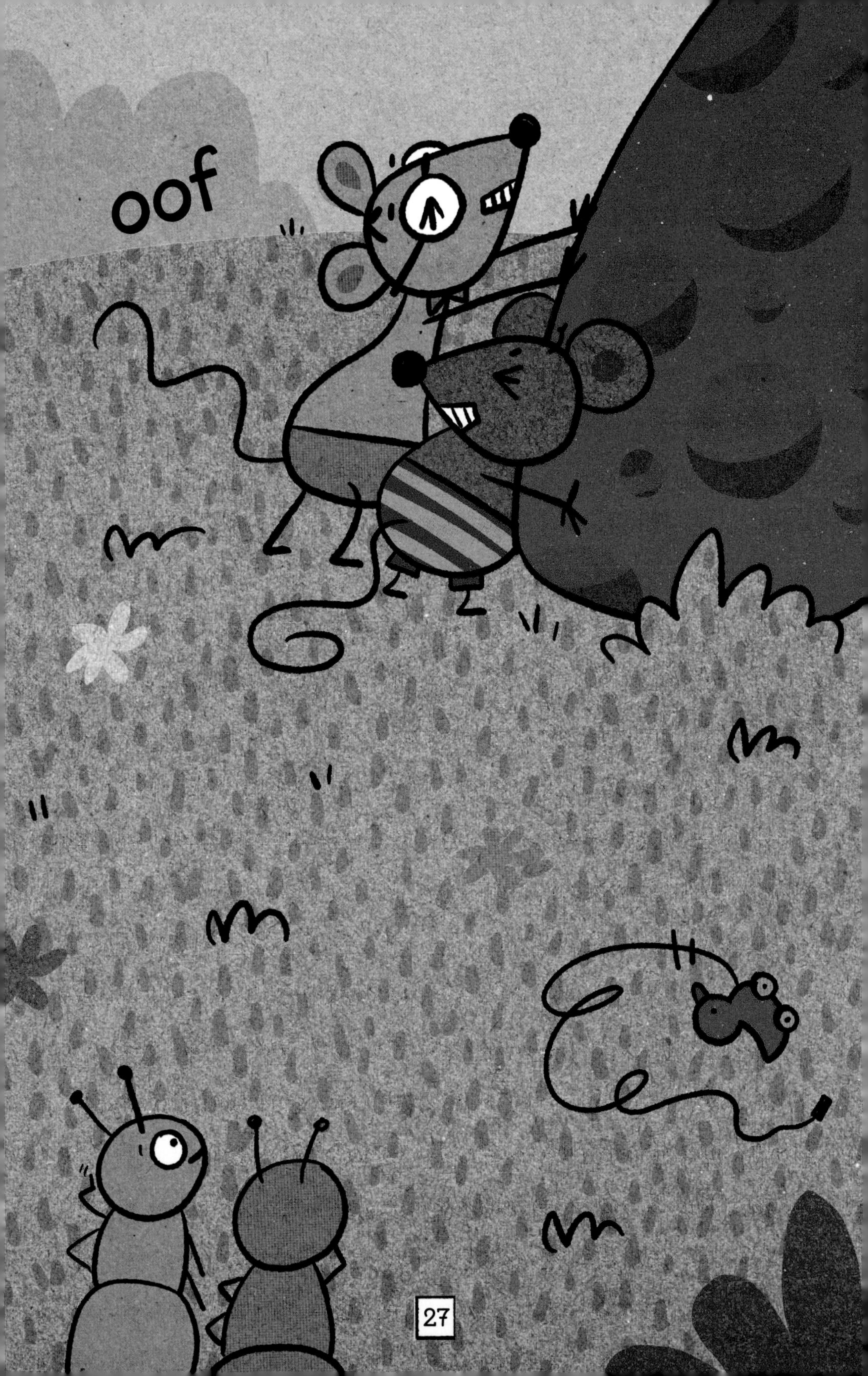
oof

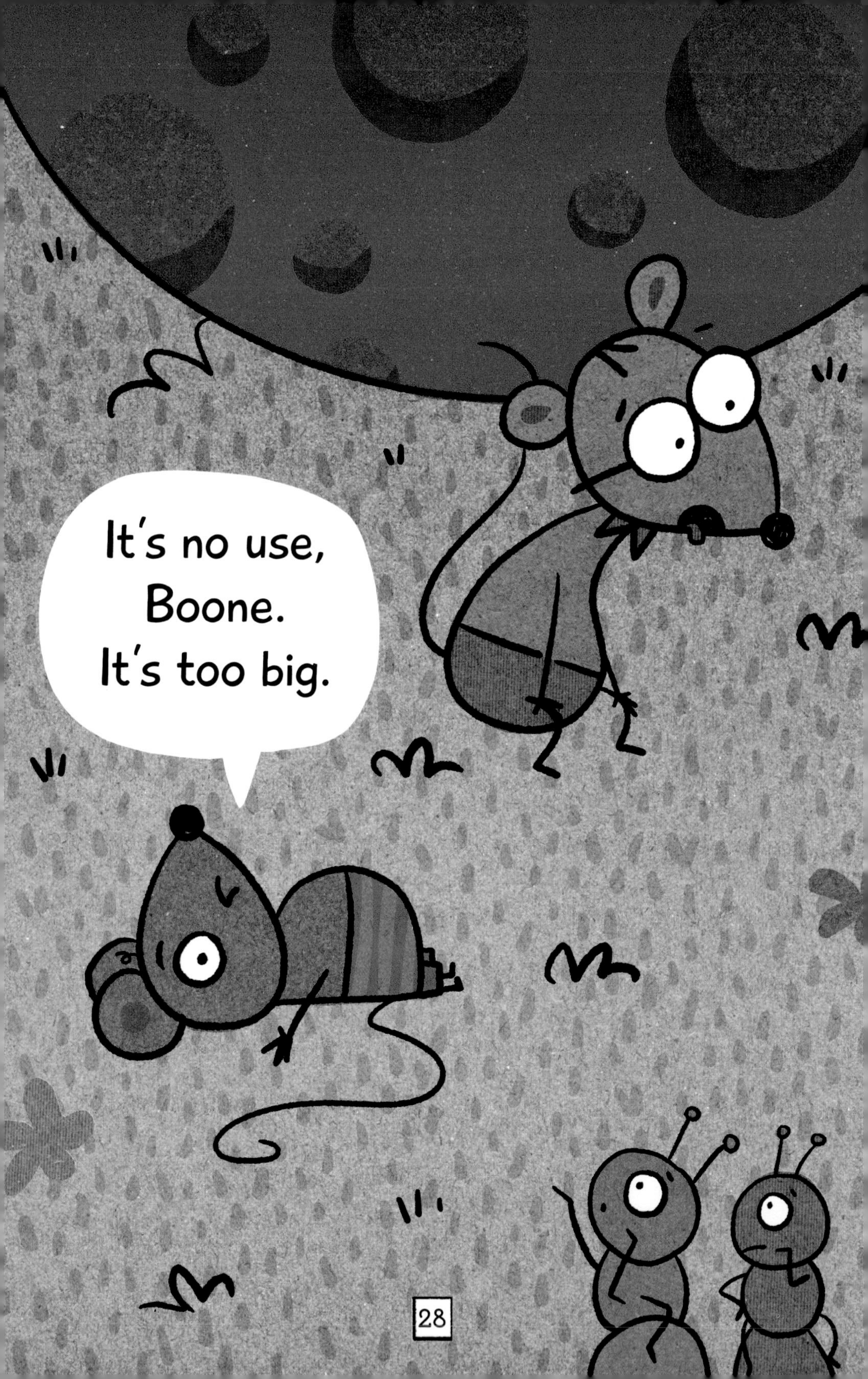
It's no use, Boone. It's too big.

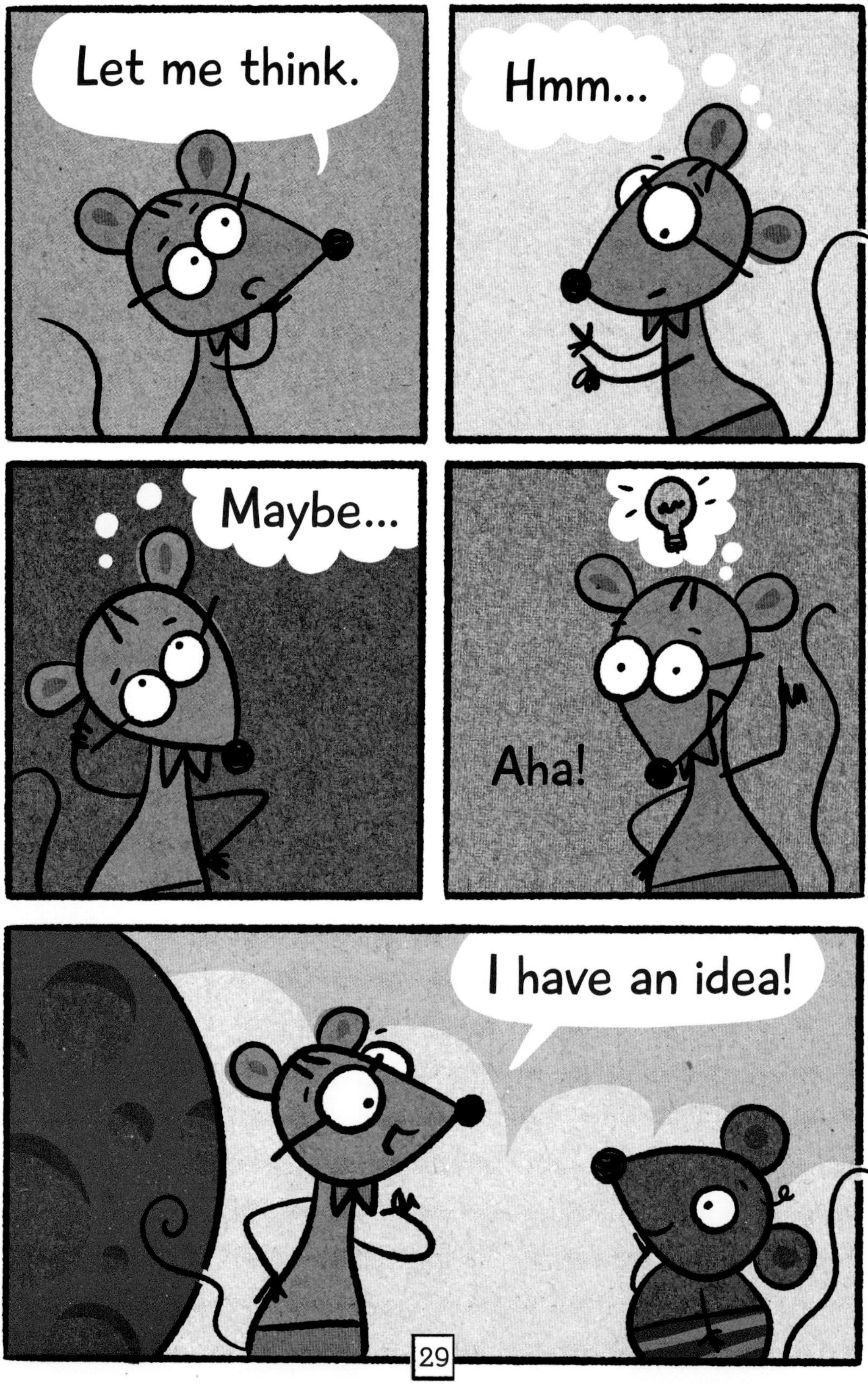
Let me think.
Hmm...
Maybe...
Aha!
I have an idea!

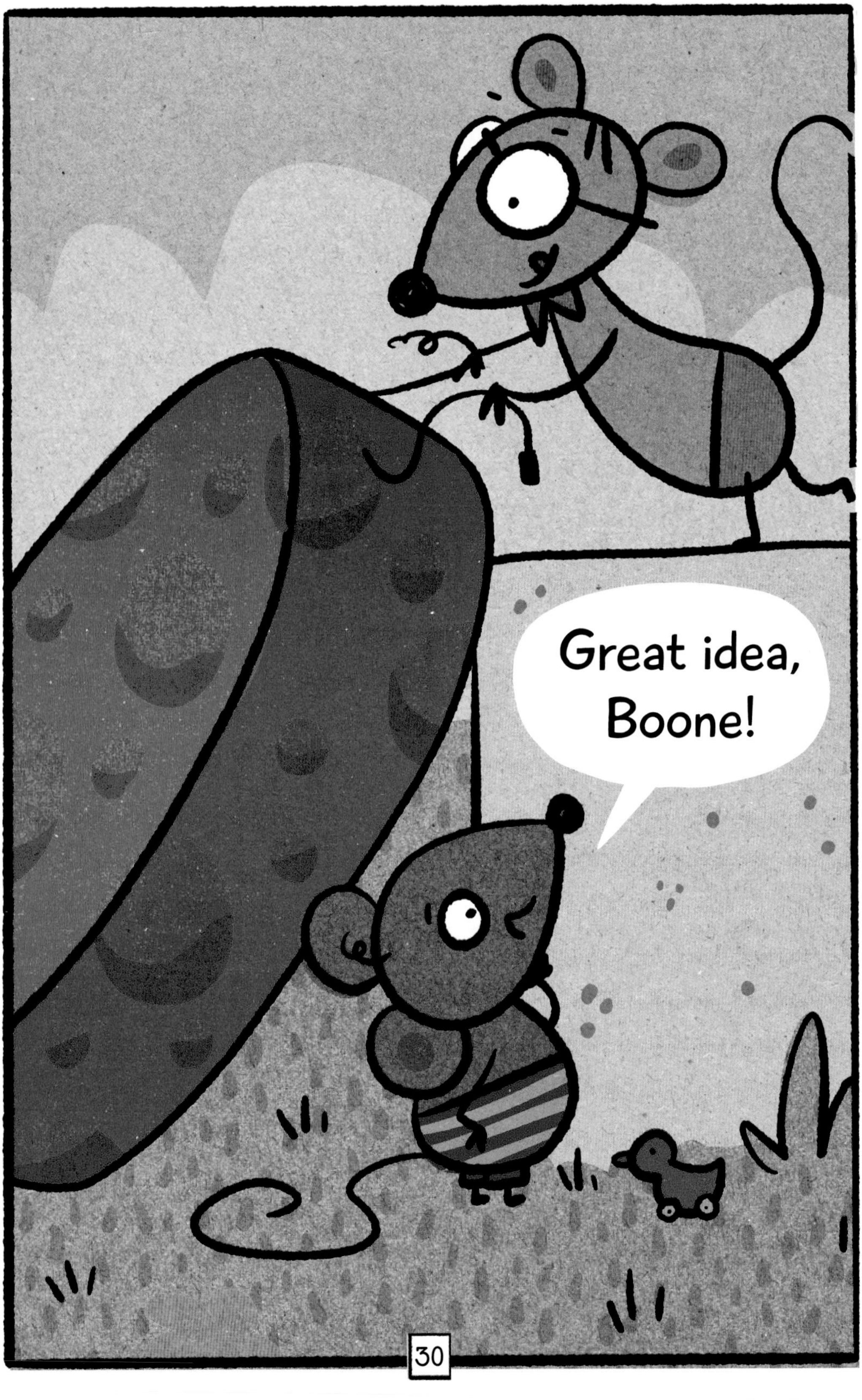
Great idea,
Boone!

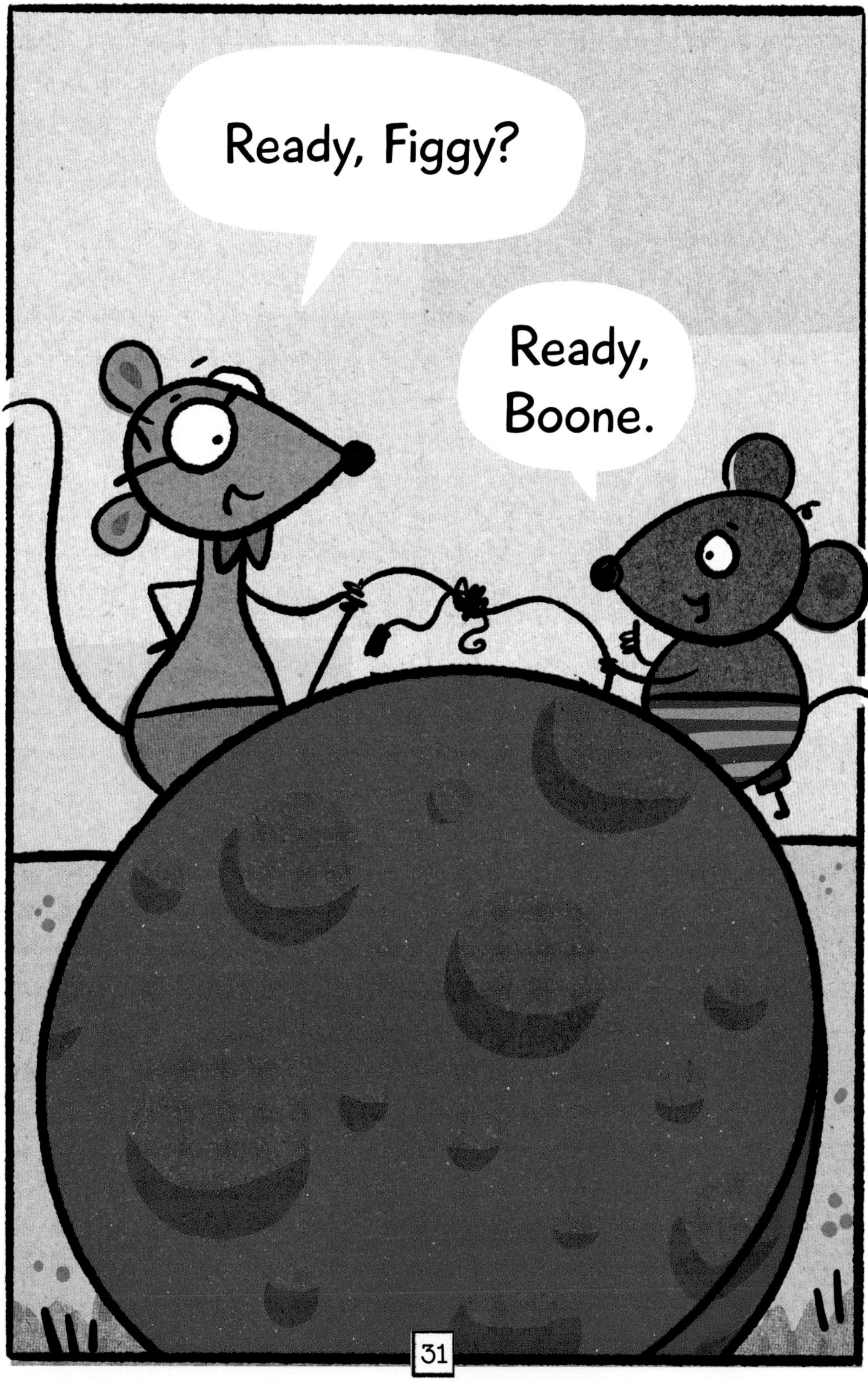
Ready, Figgy?
Ready, Boone.

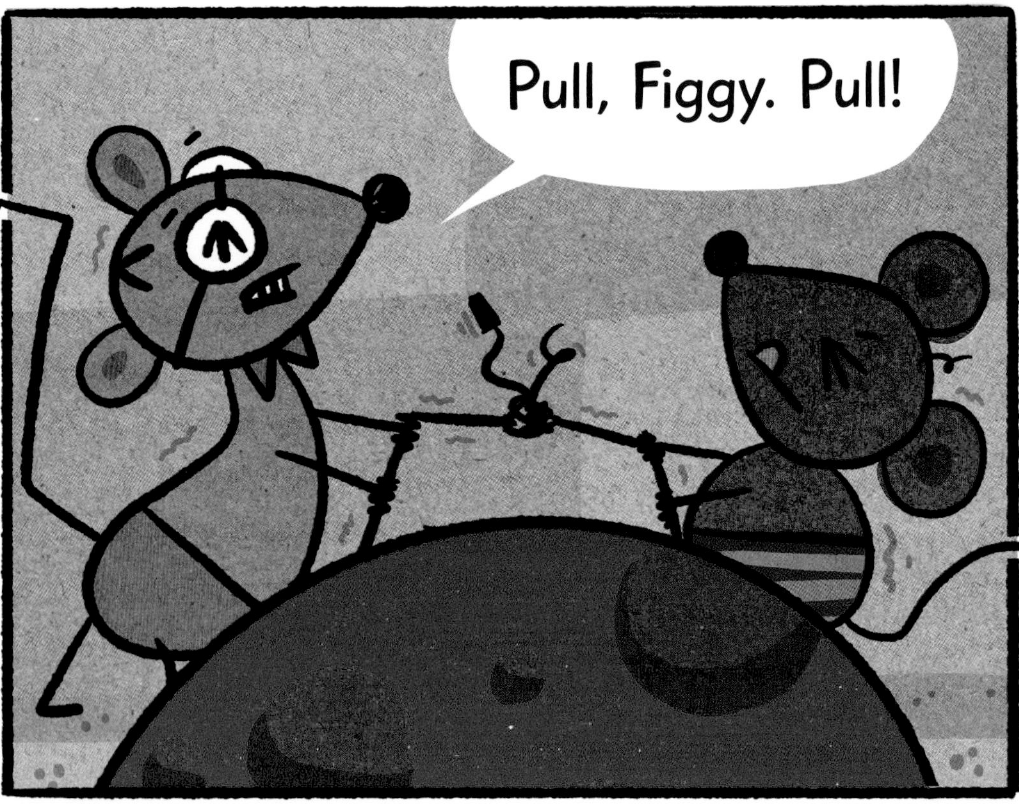
Pull, Figgy. Pull!

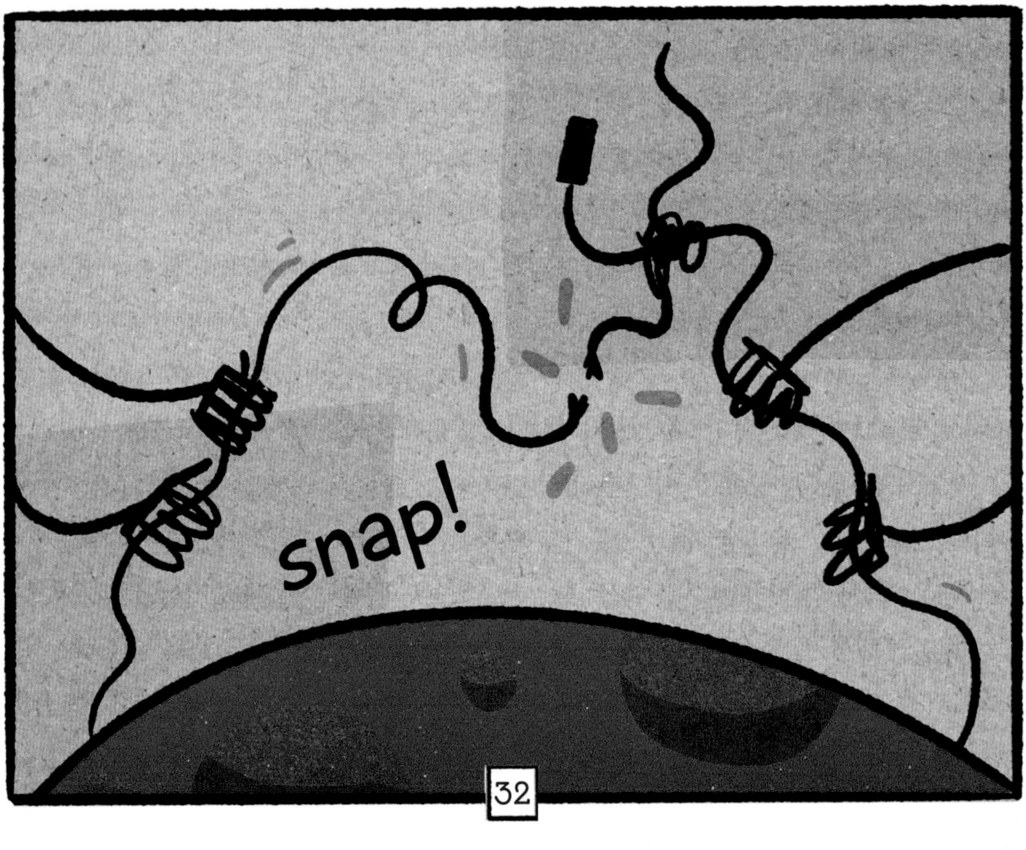
snap!

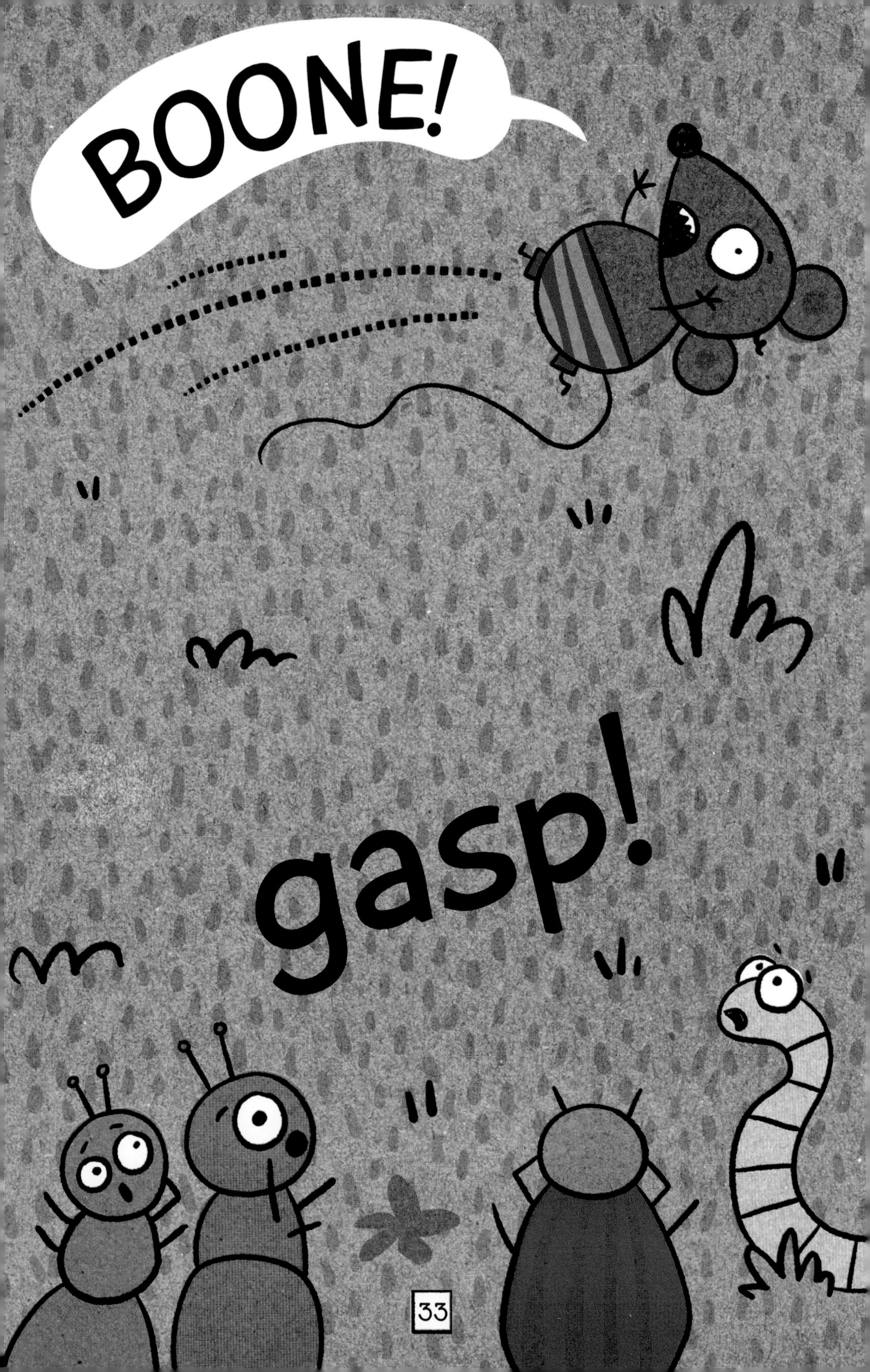
BOONE!
gasp!

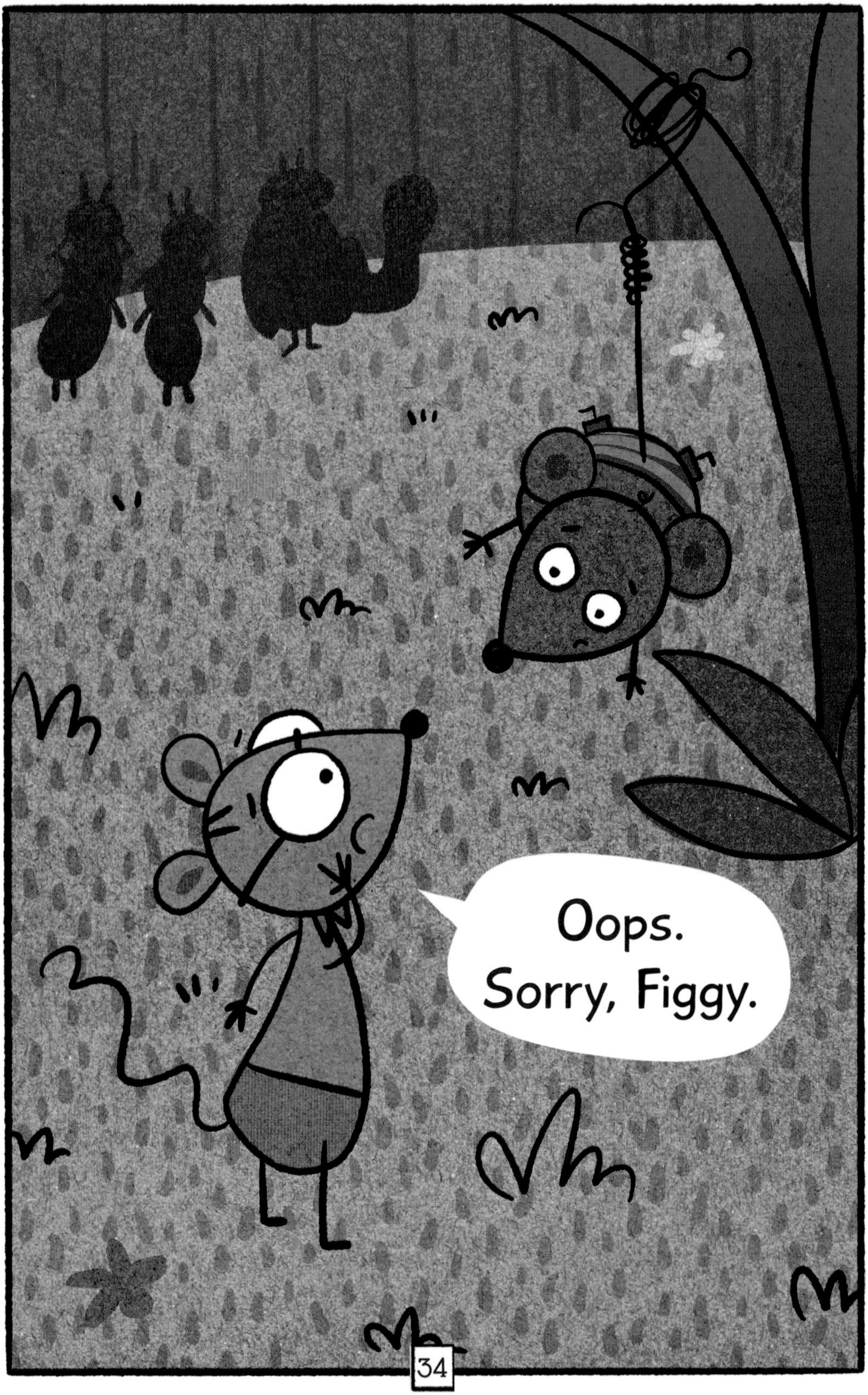
Oops.
Sorry, Figgy.

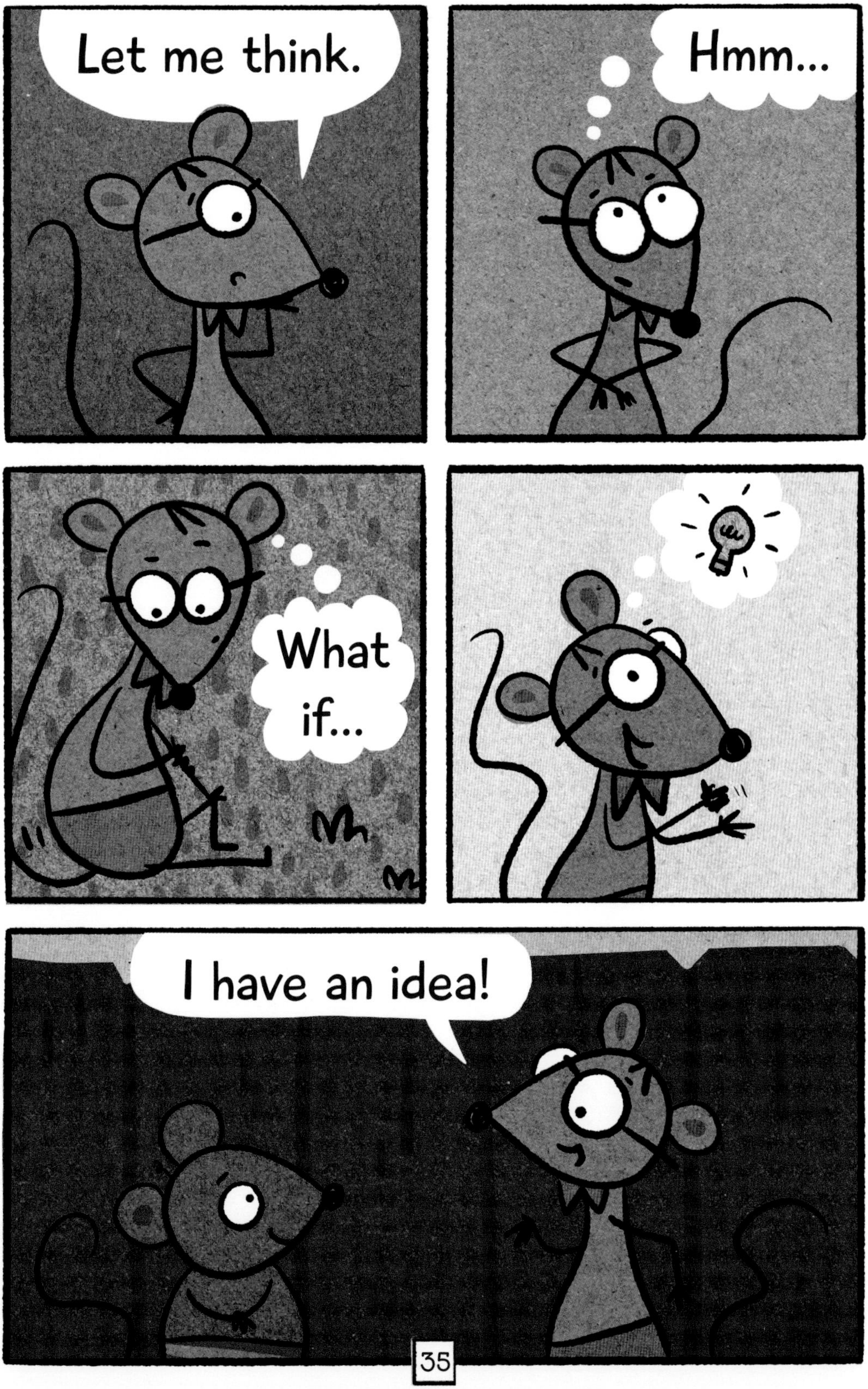
Let me think.
Hmm...
What if...
I have an idea!

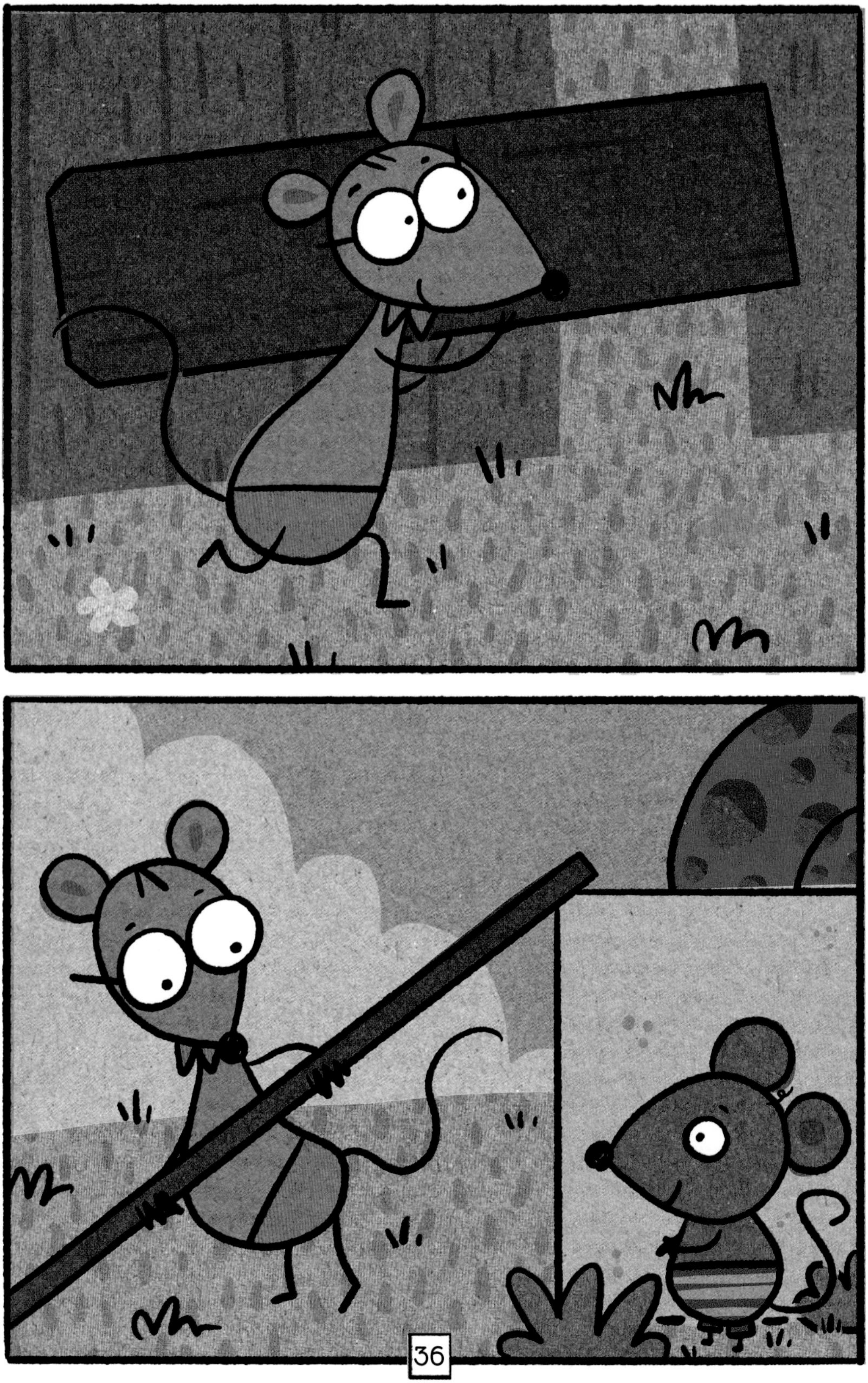

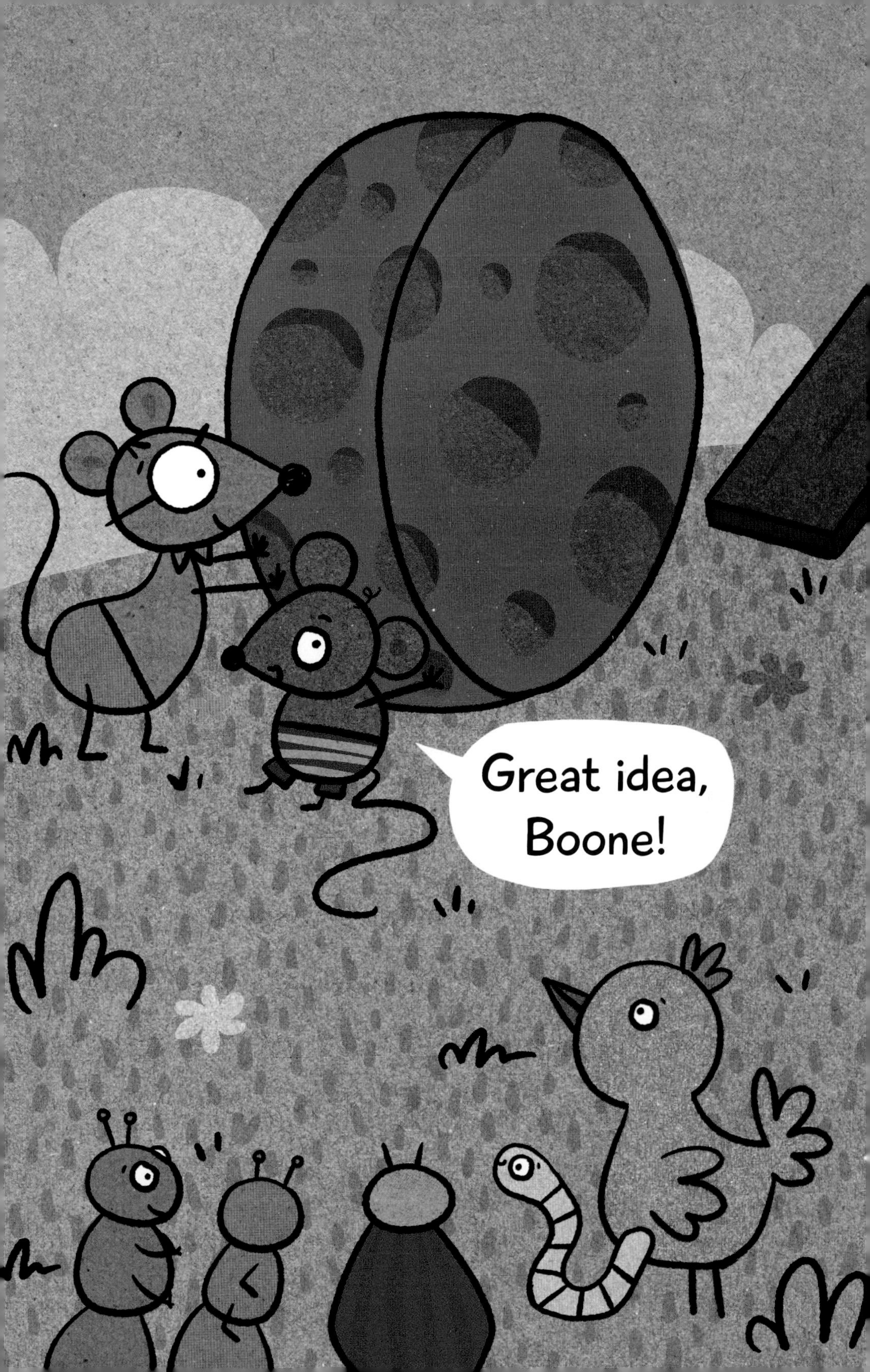
Great idea,
Boone!

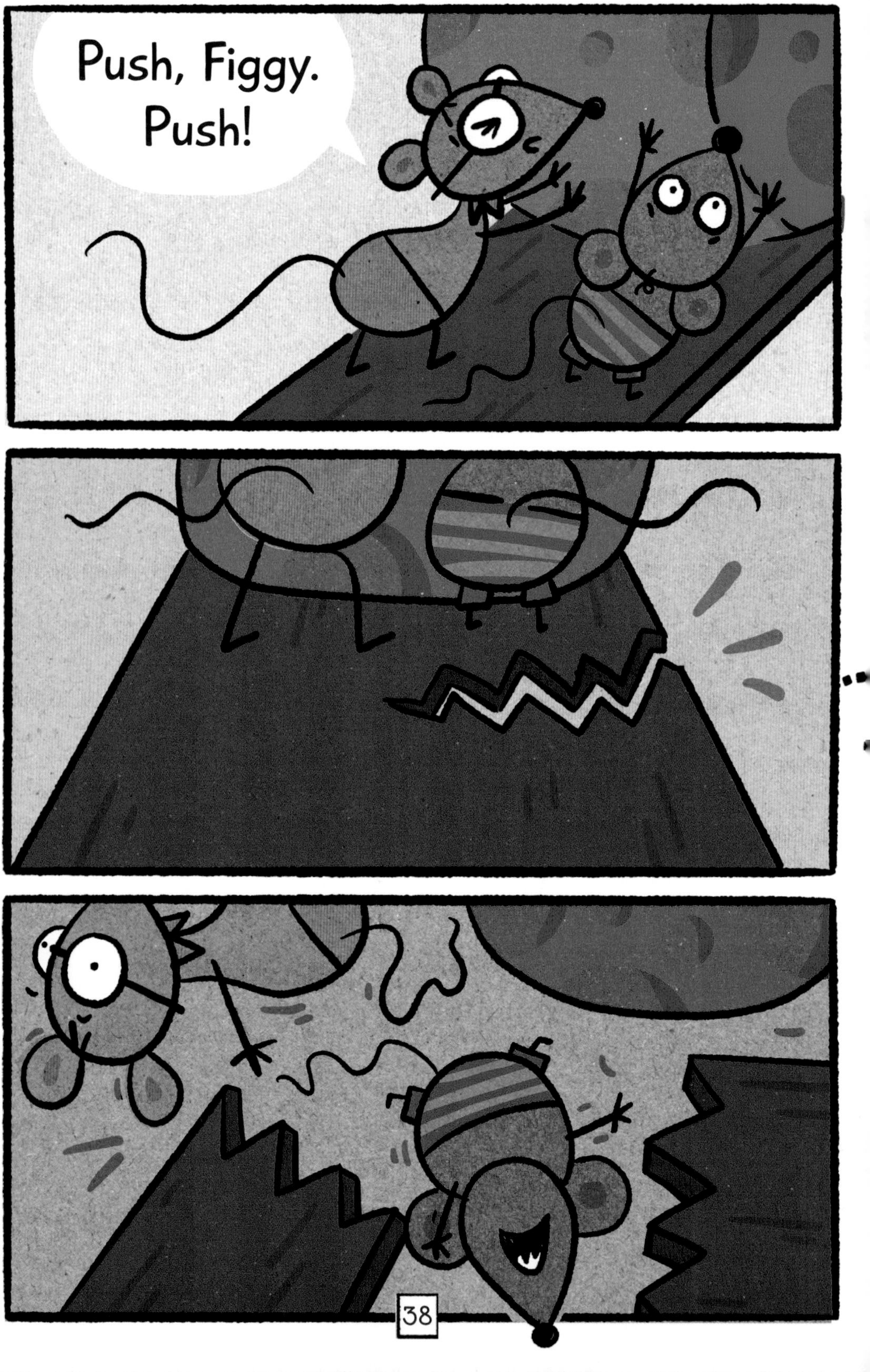
Push, Figgy.
Push!

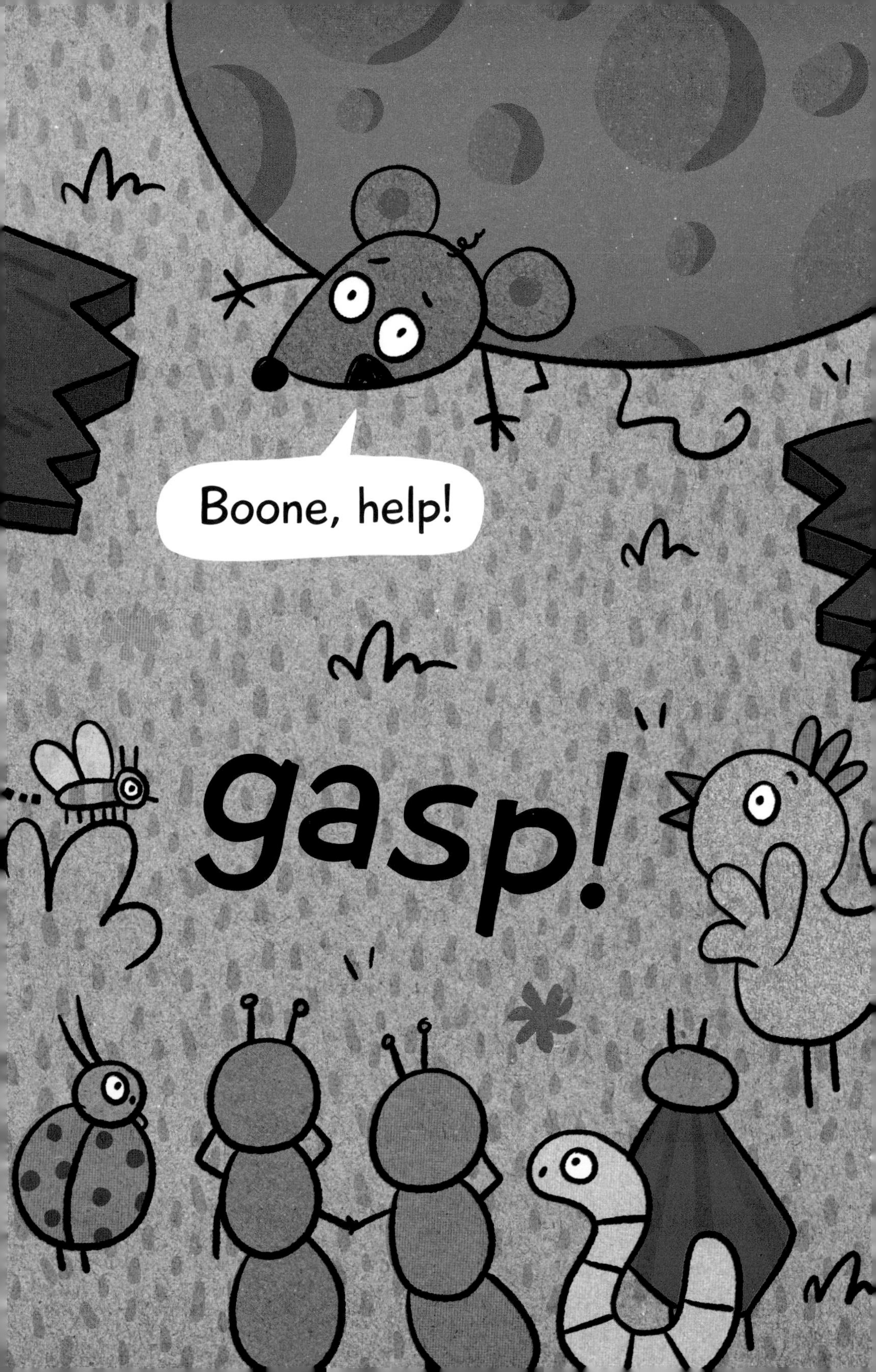
Boone, help!
gasp!

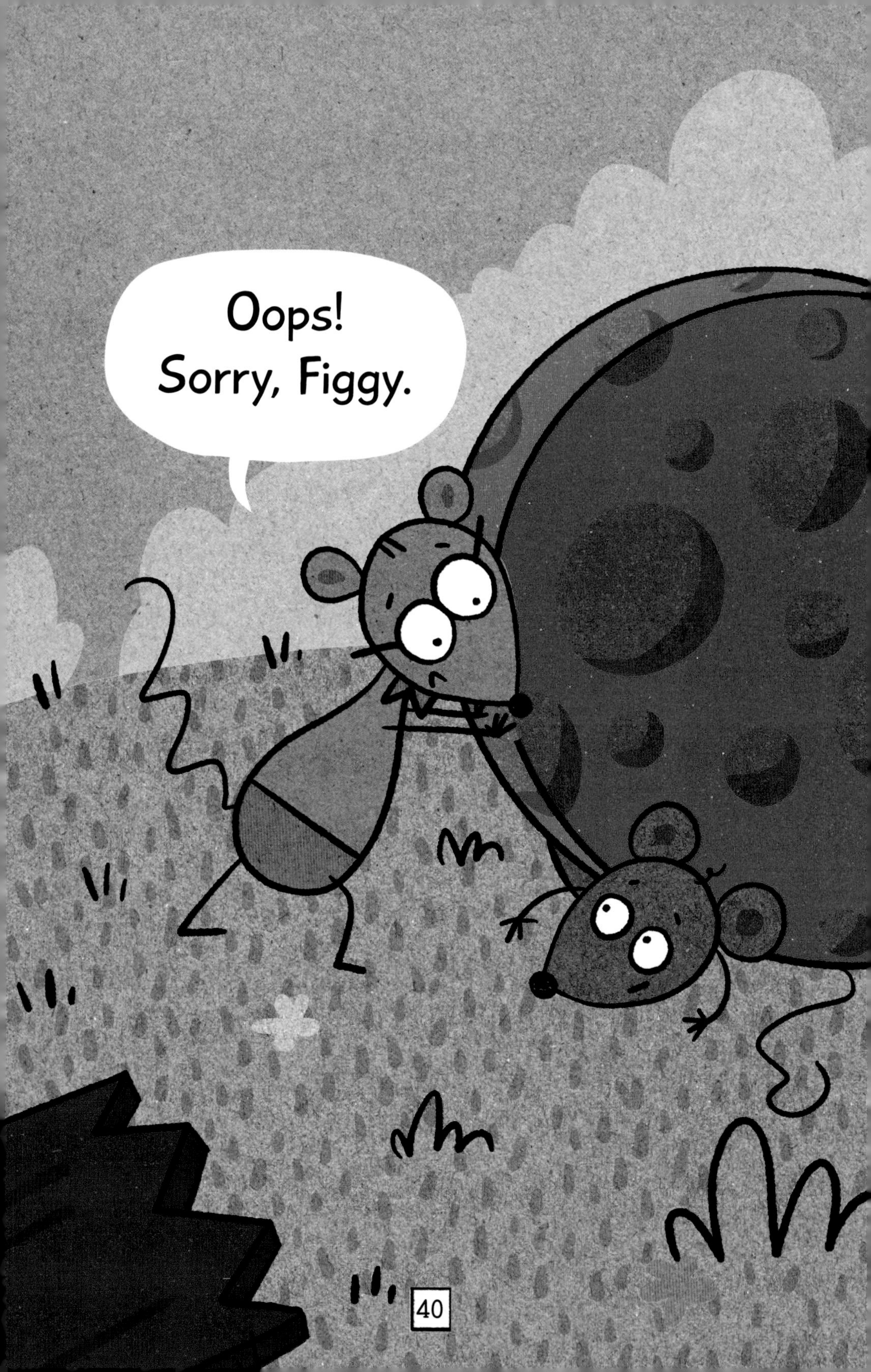
Oops! Sorry, Figgy.

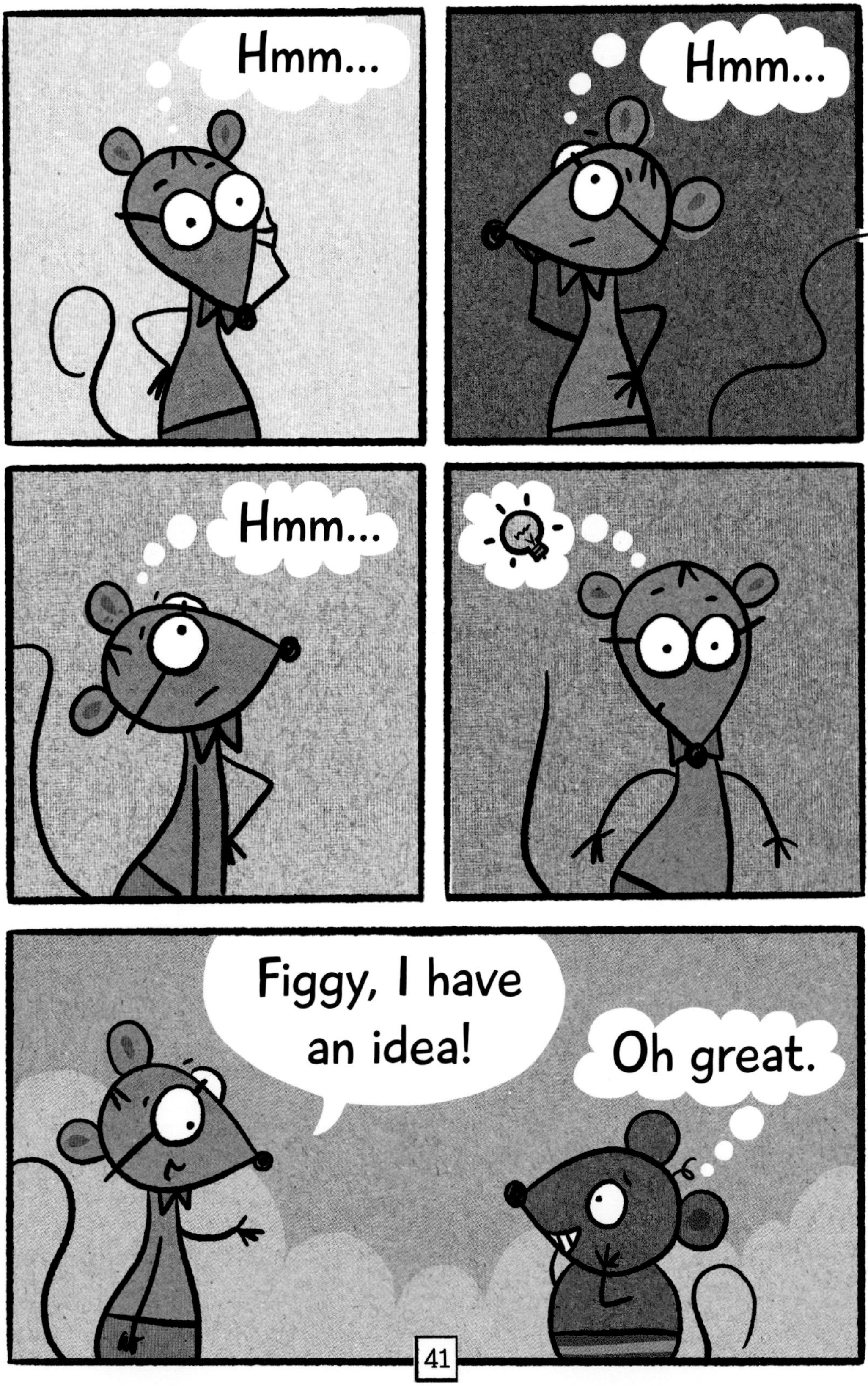
Hmm...
Hmm...
Hmm...
Figgy, I have an idea!
Oh great.

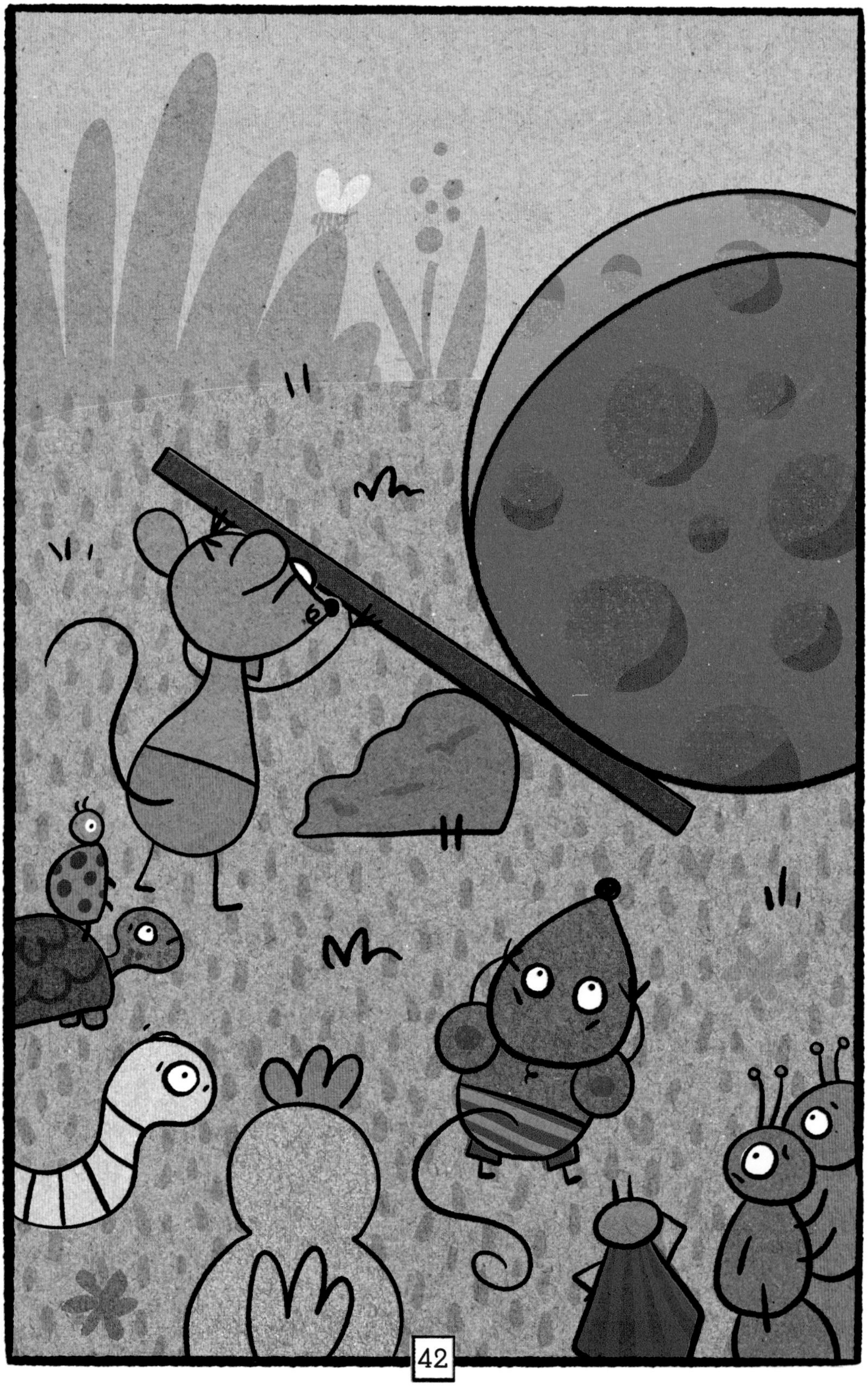

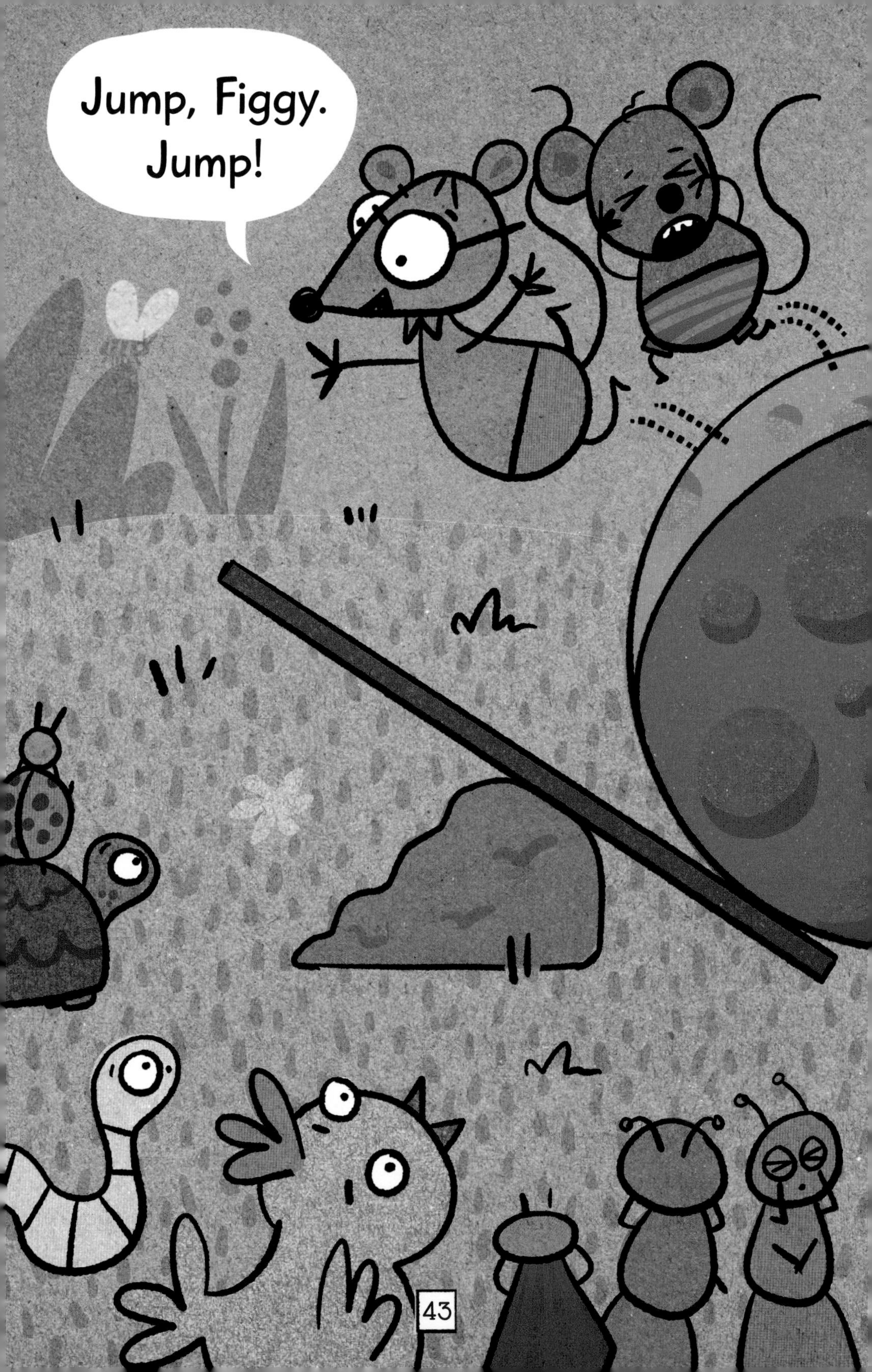
Jump, Figgy. Jump!

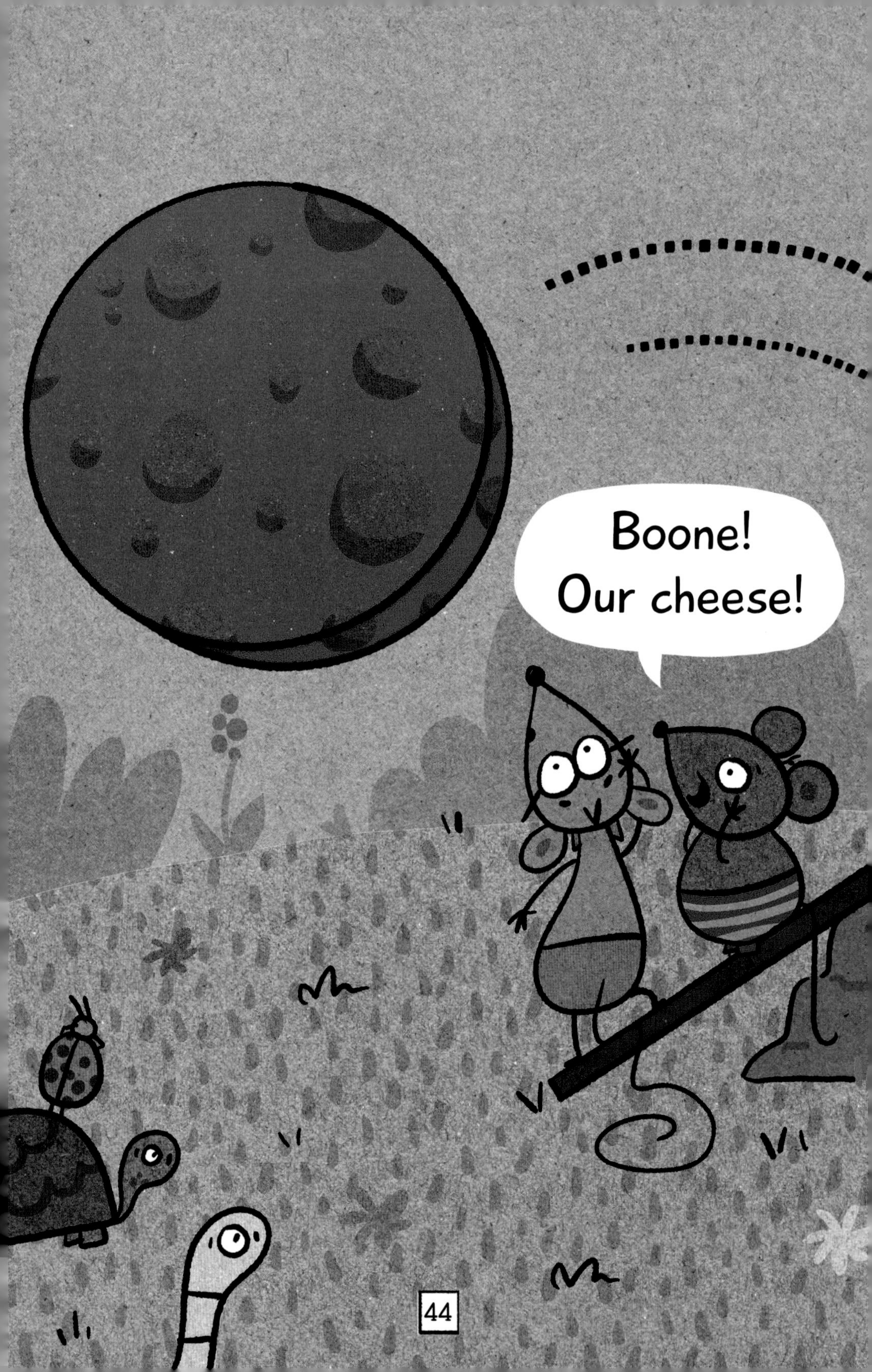
Boone!
Our cheese!

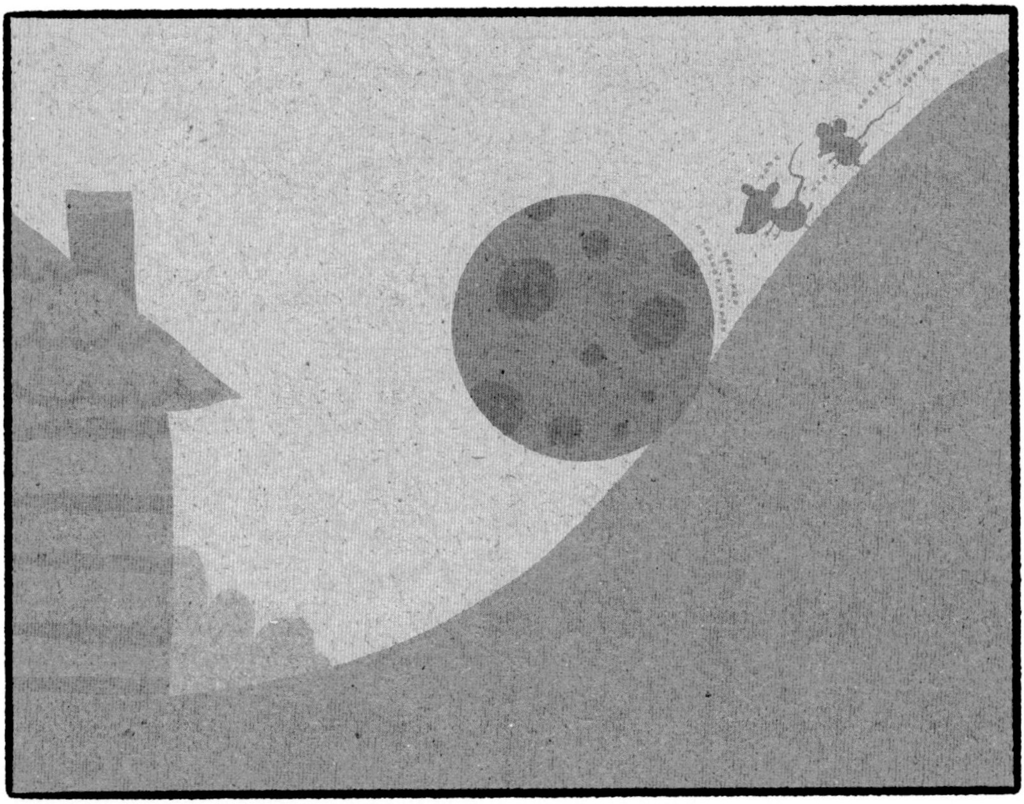

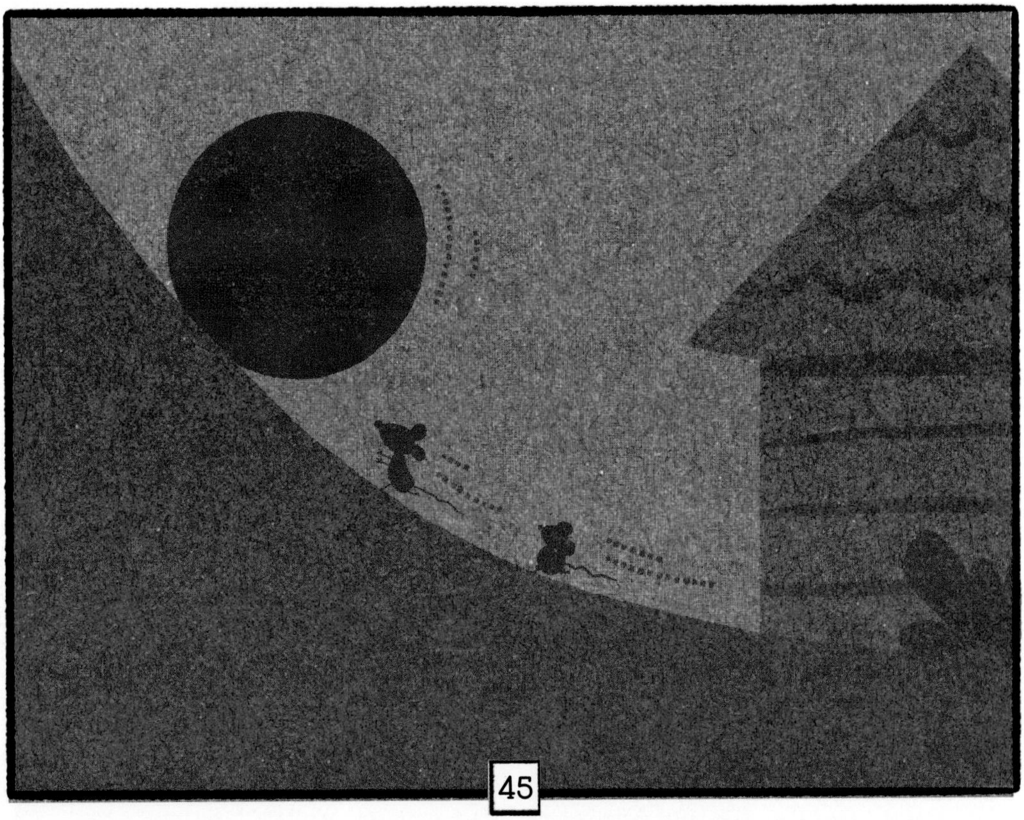

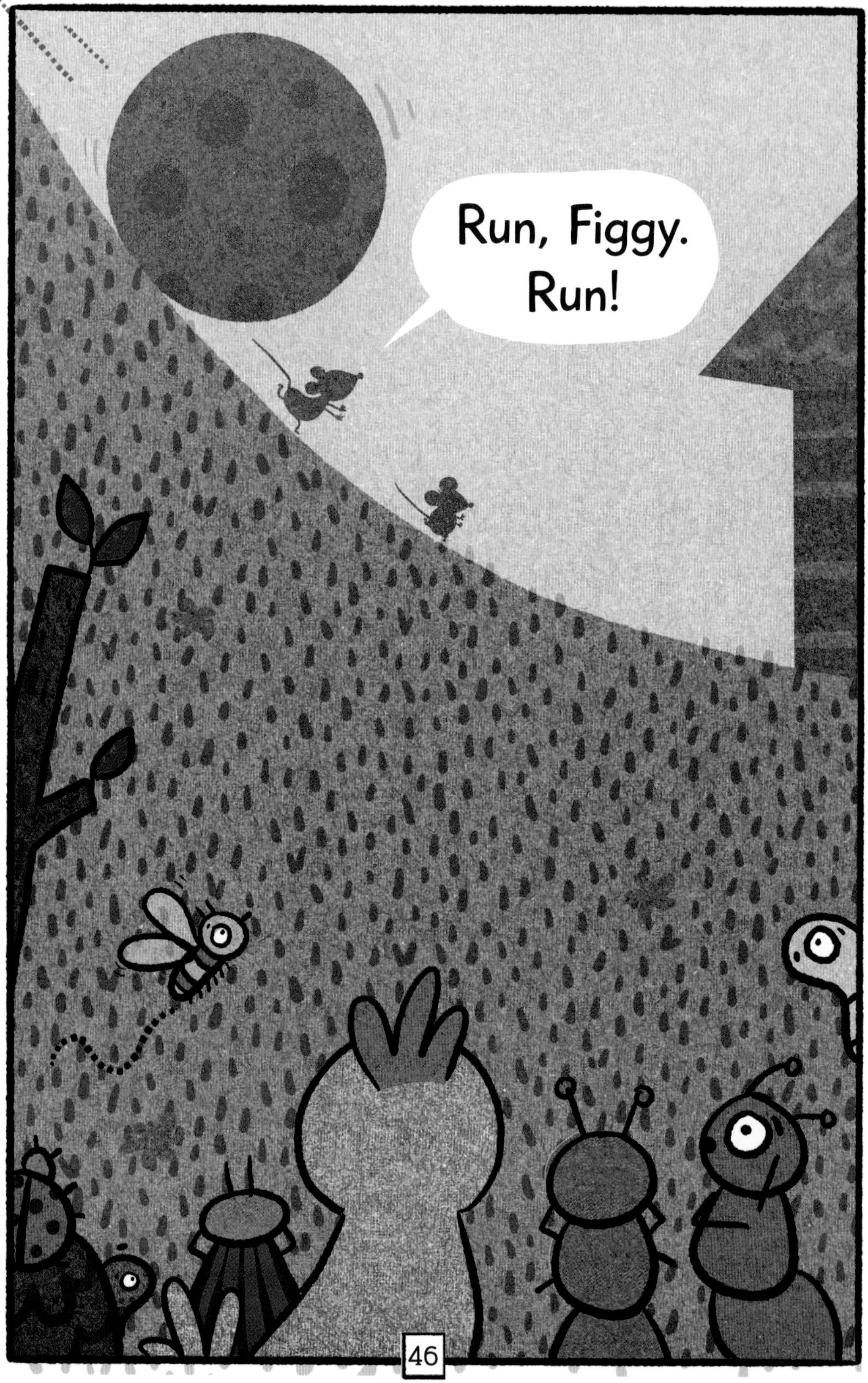
Run, Figgy.
Run!

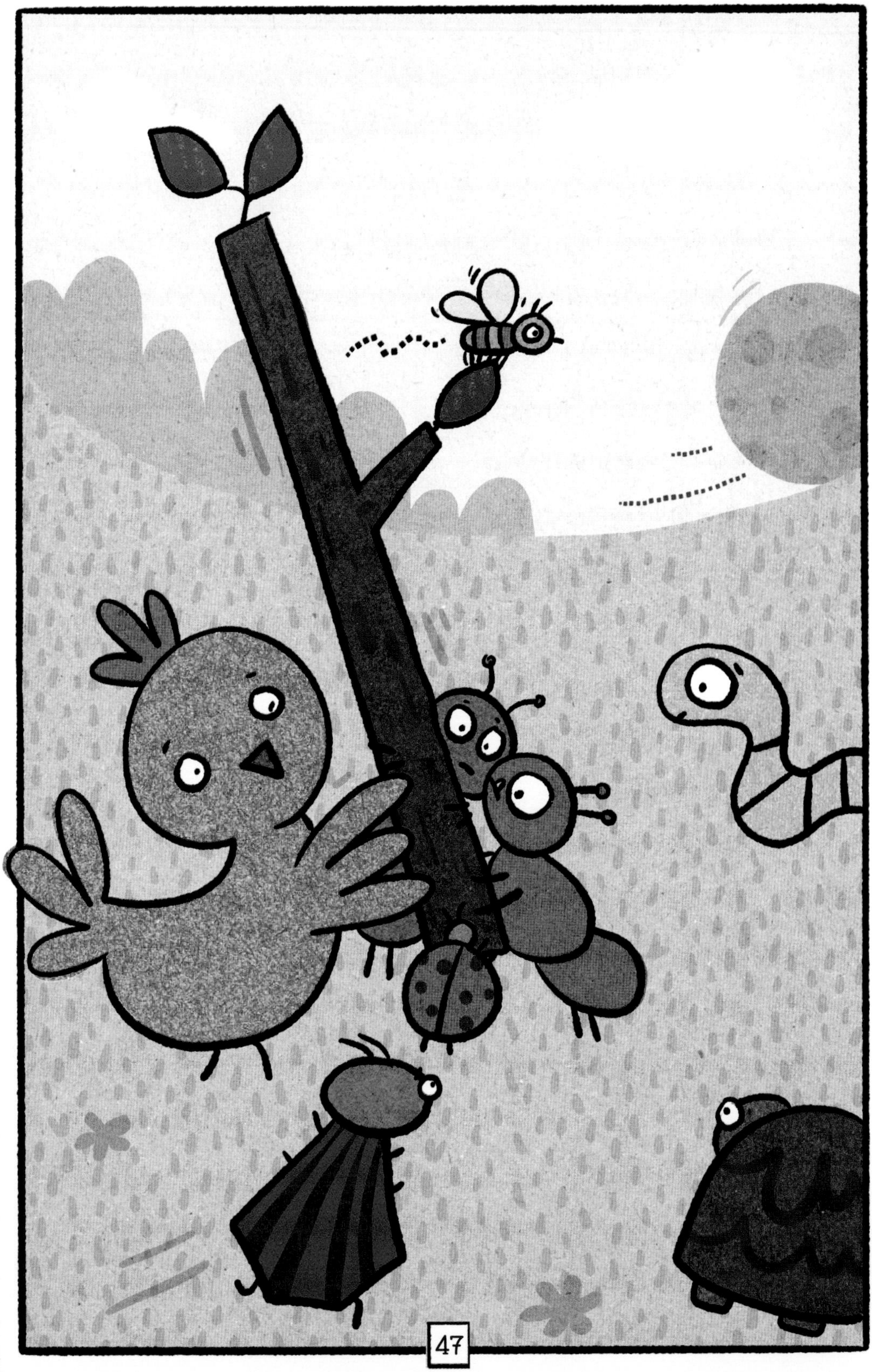

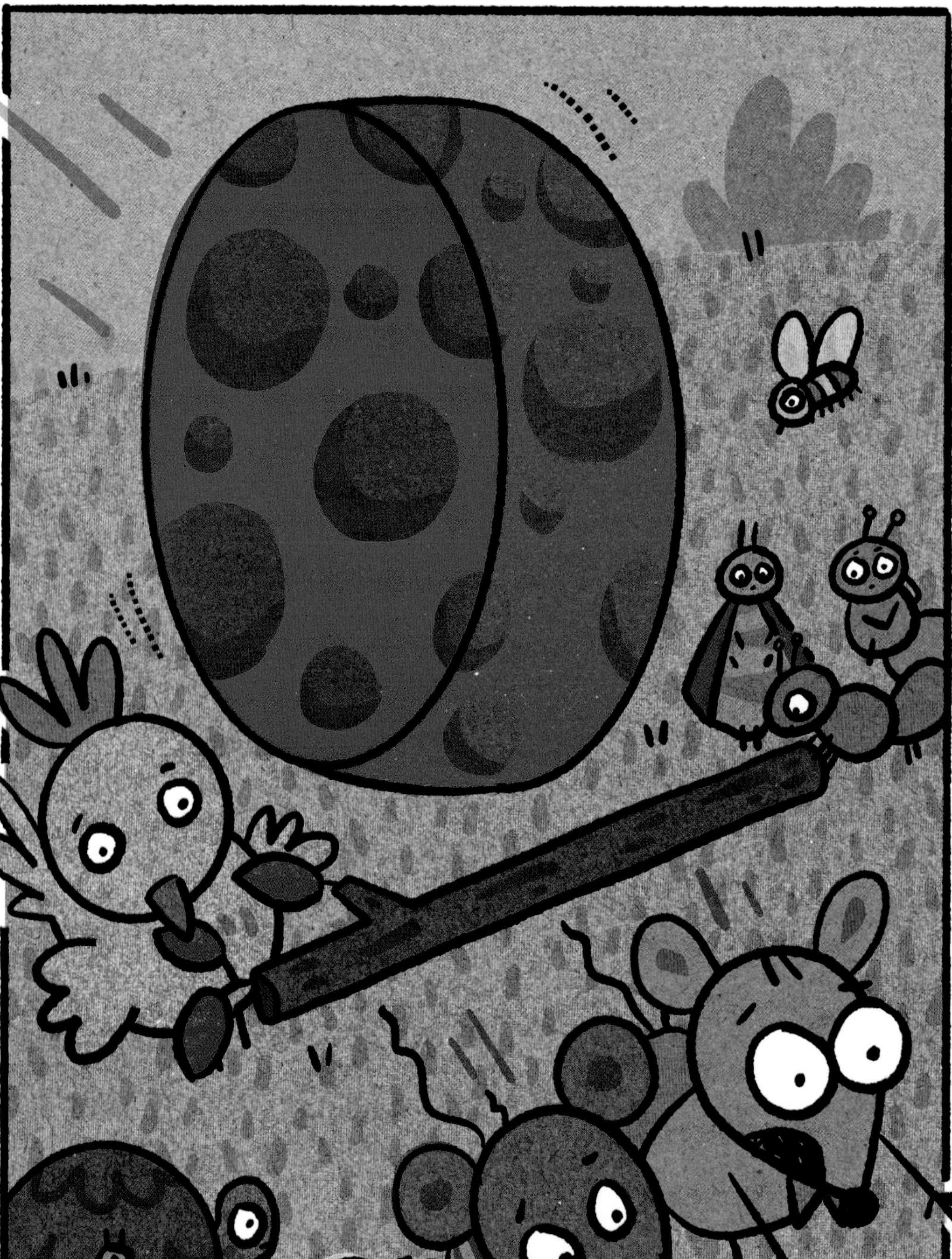

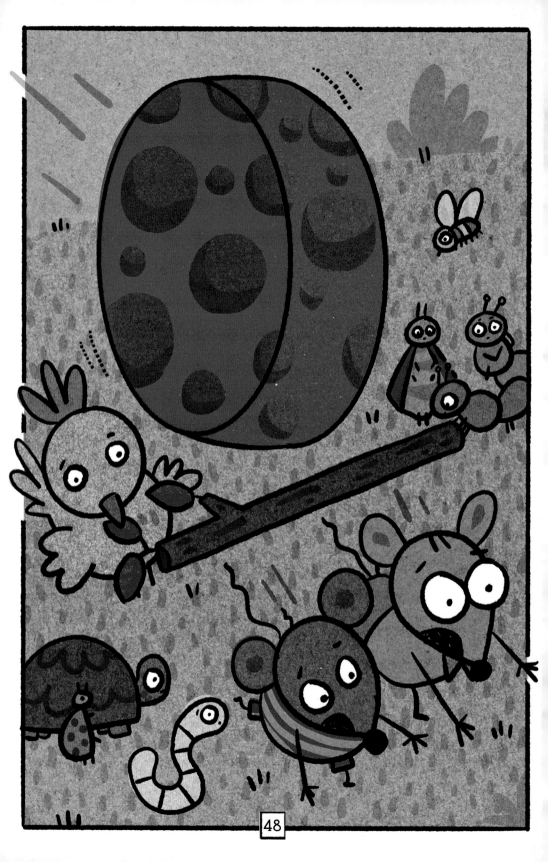

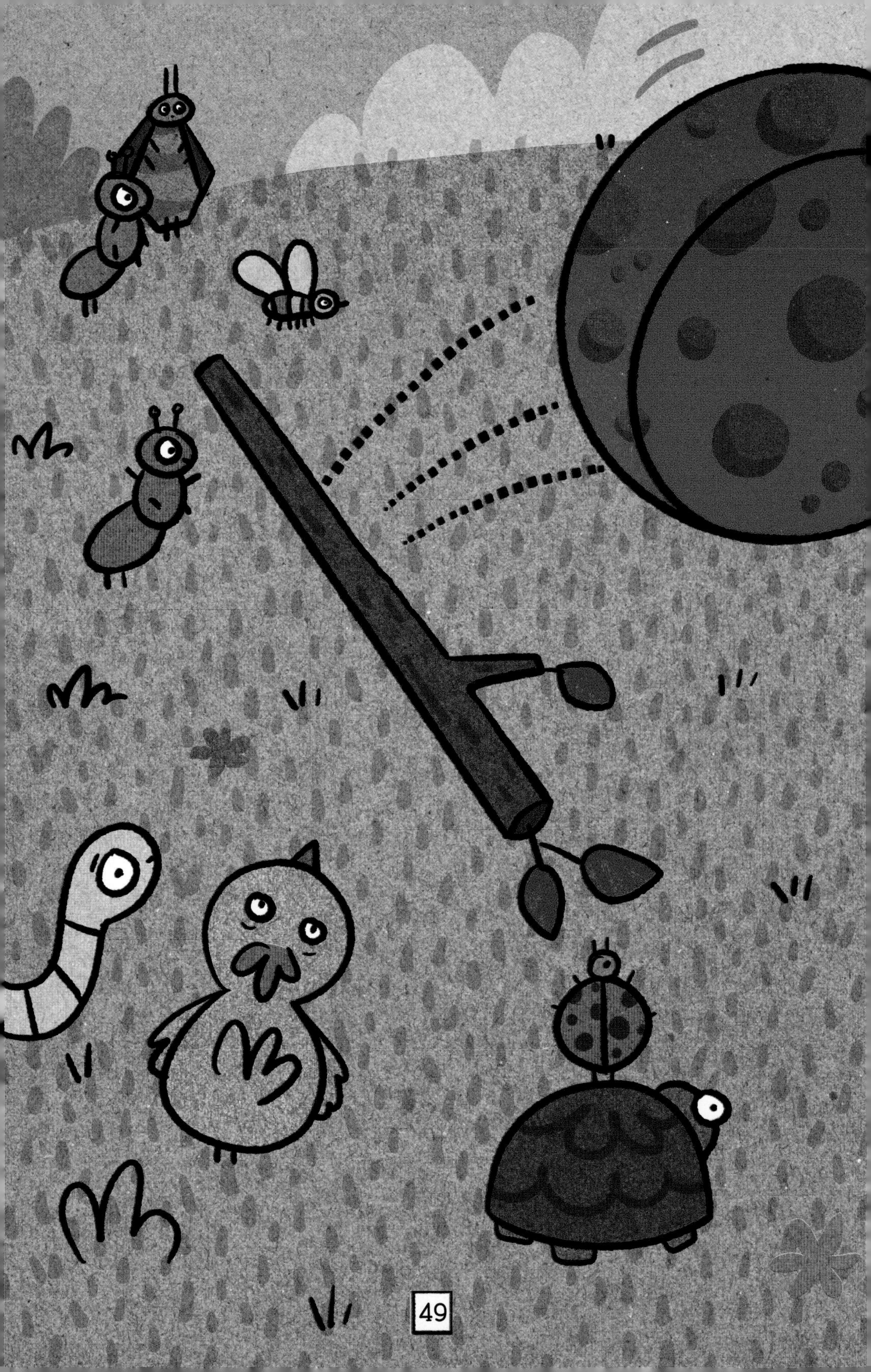

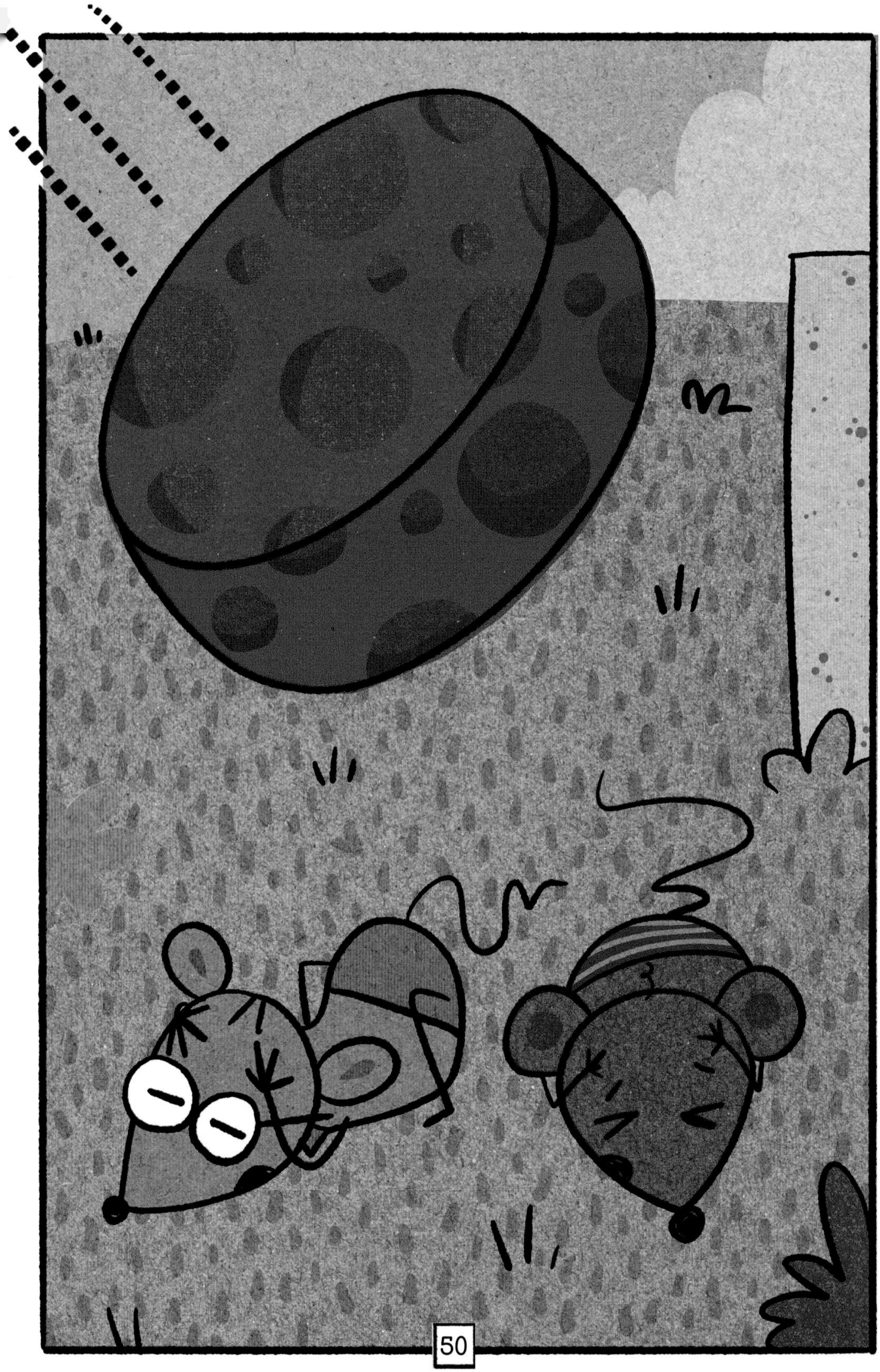

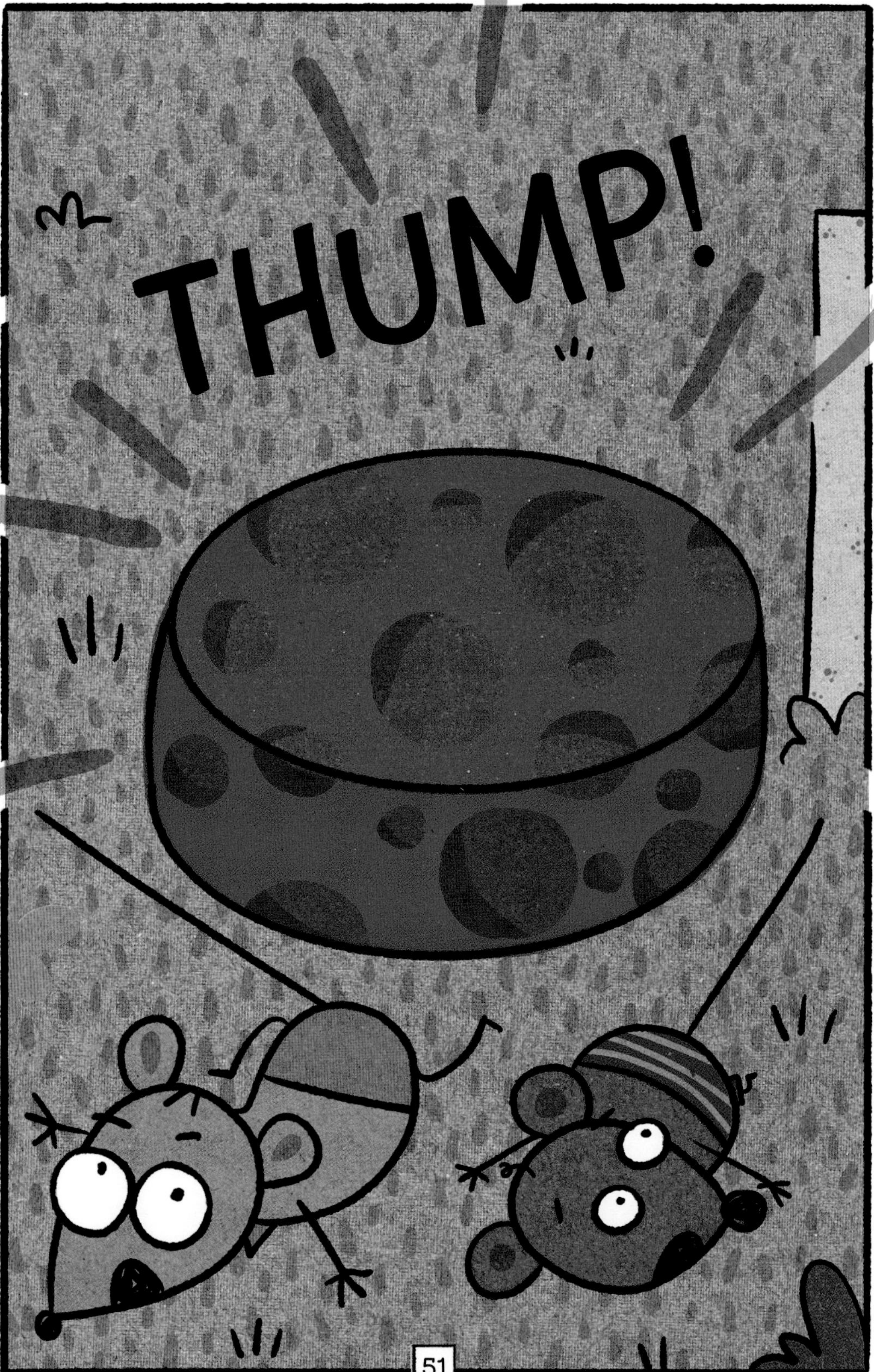
THUMP!

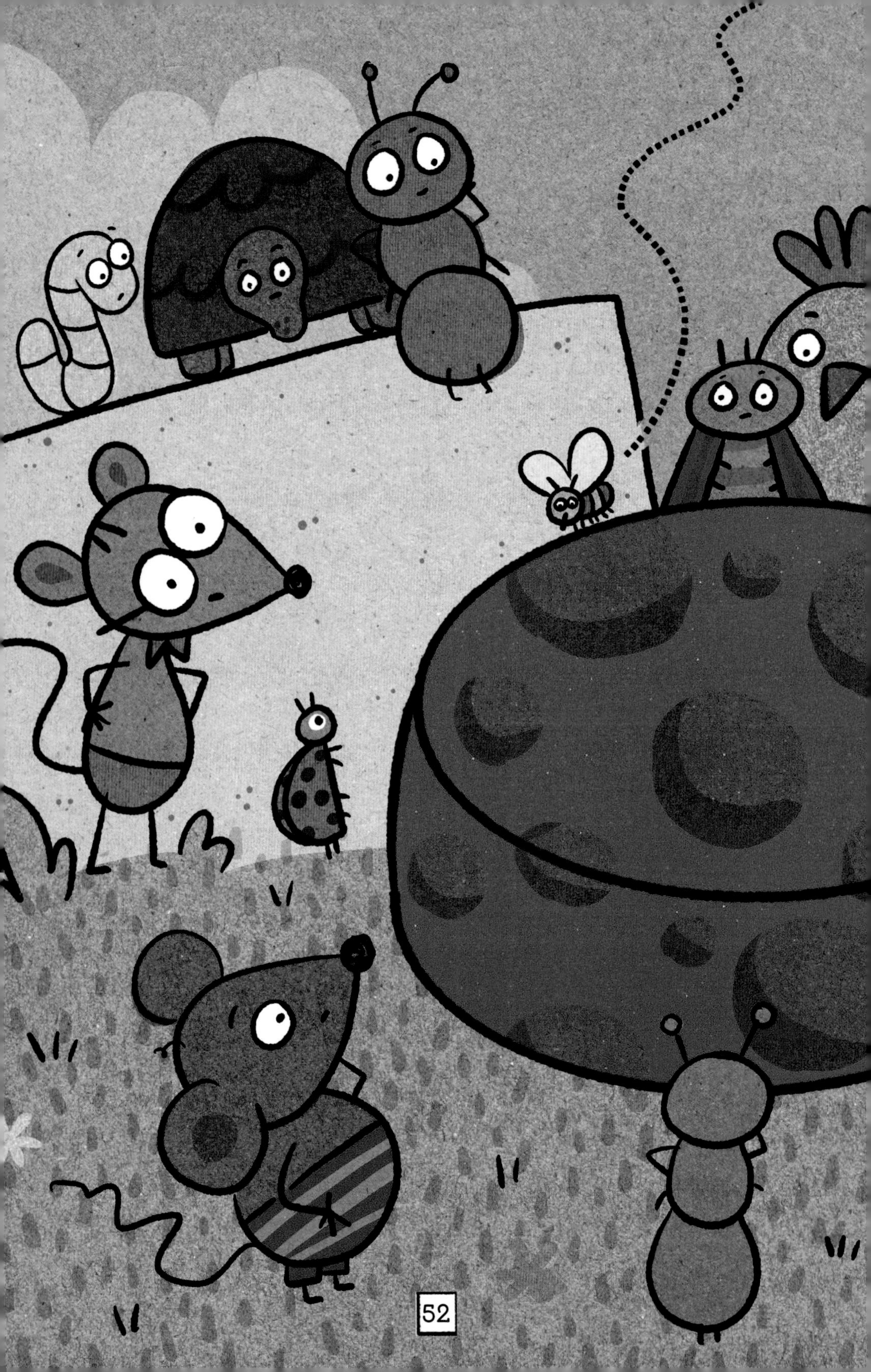

Boone's Thought for the Day

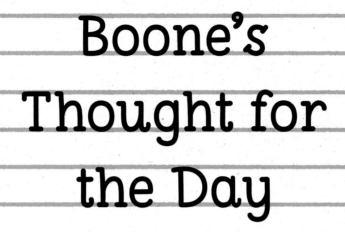

If at first you don't succeed, try science.

Figgy's Thought for the Day

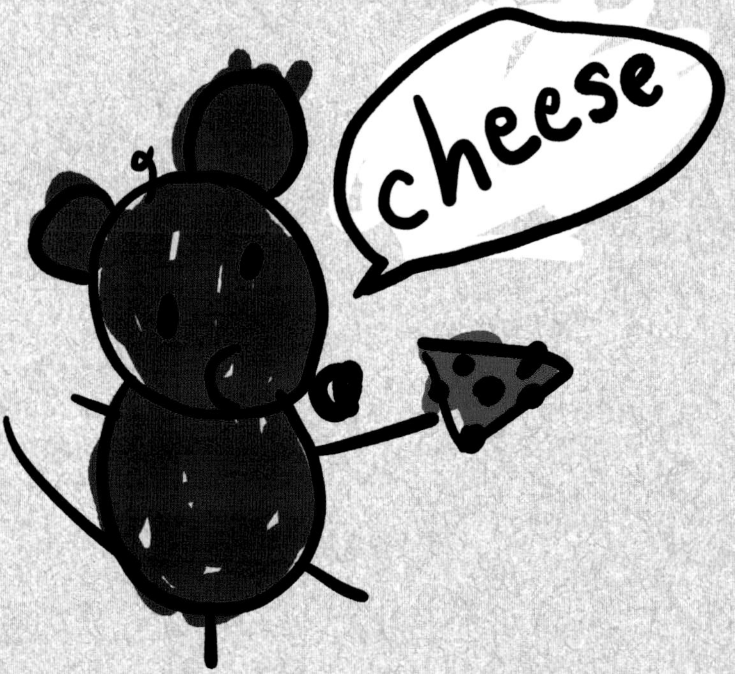
cheese

Chapter 3

A Cheesy Idea

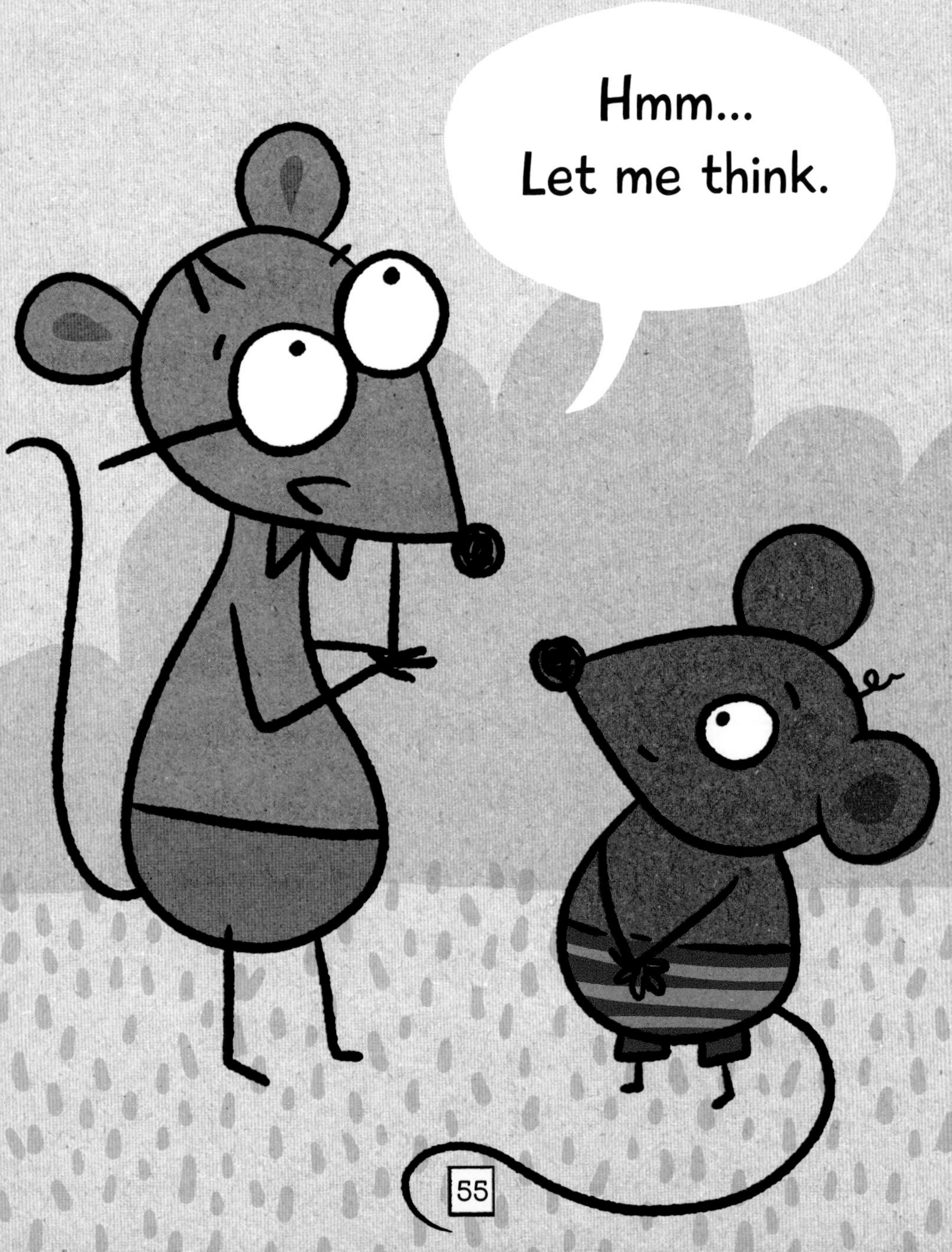
Hmm...
Let me think.

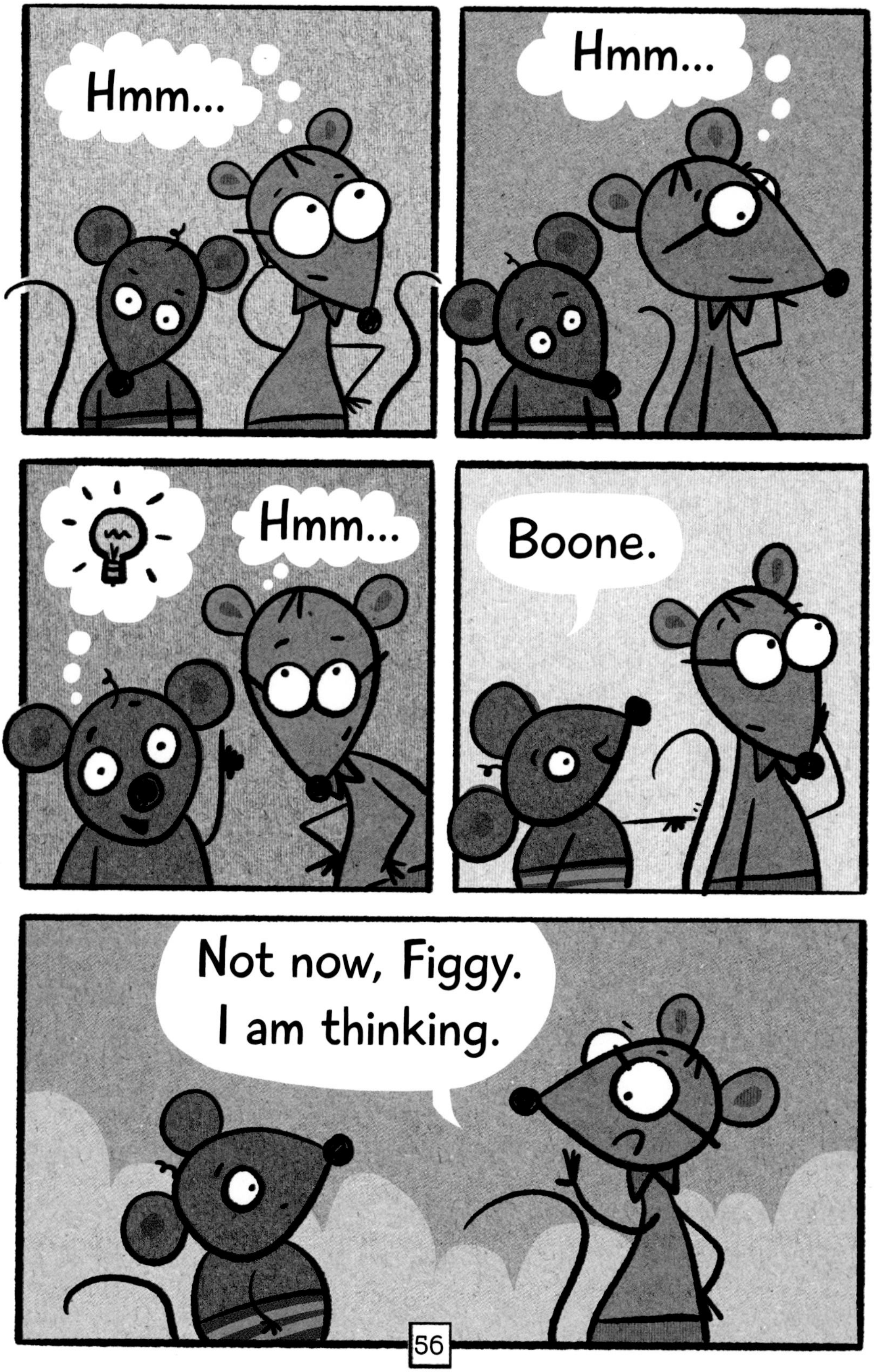
Hmm...
Hmm...
Hmm...
Boone.
Not now, Figgy.
I am thinking.

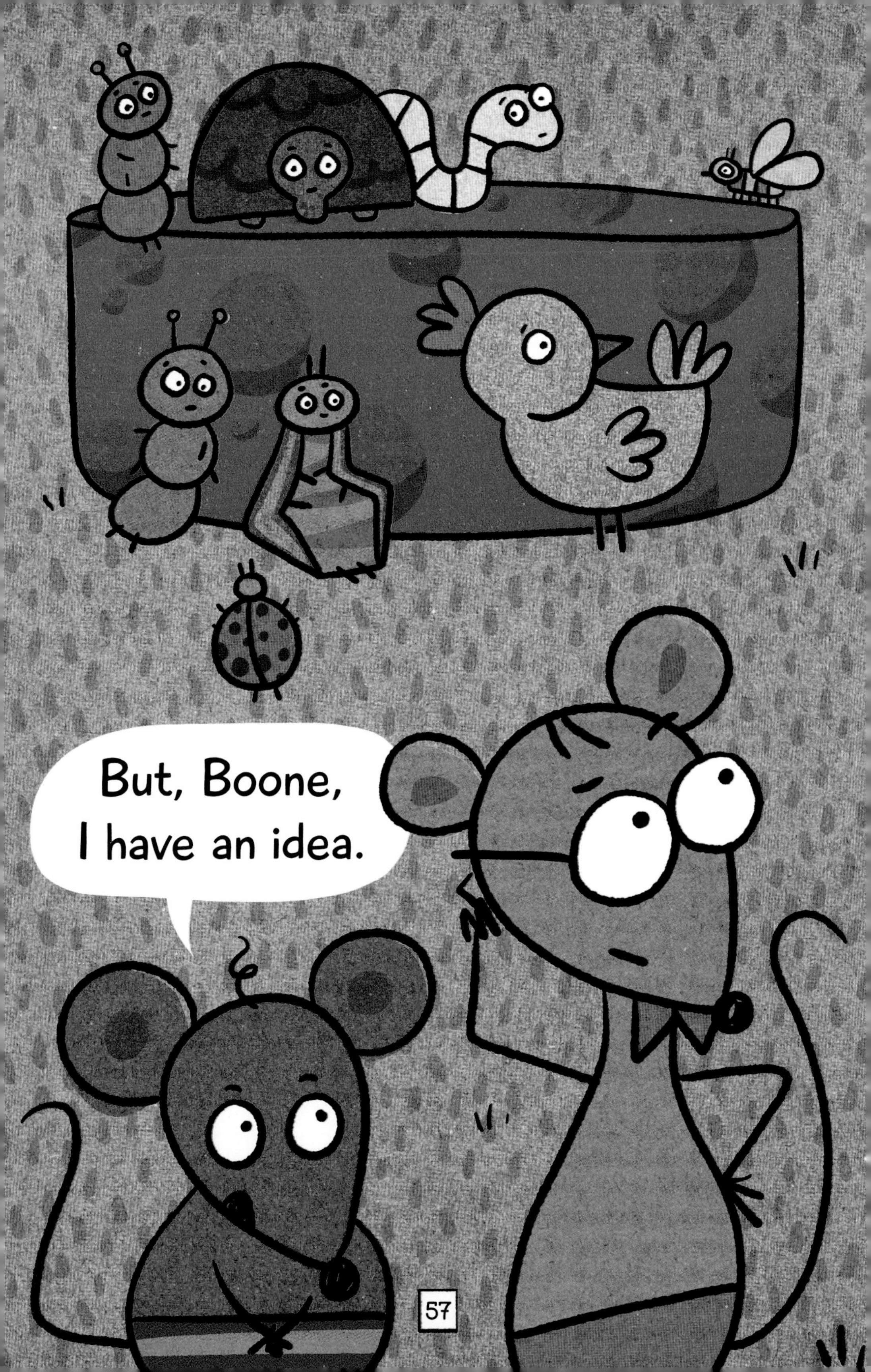
But, Boone,
I have an idea.

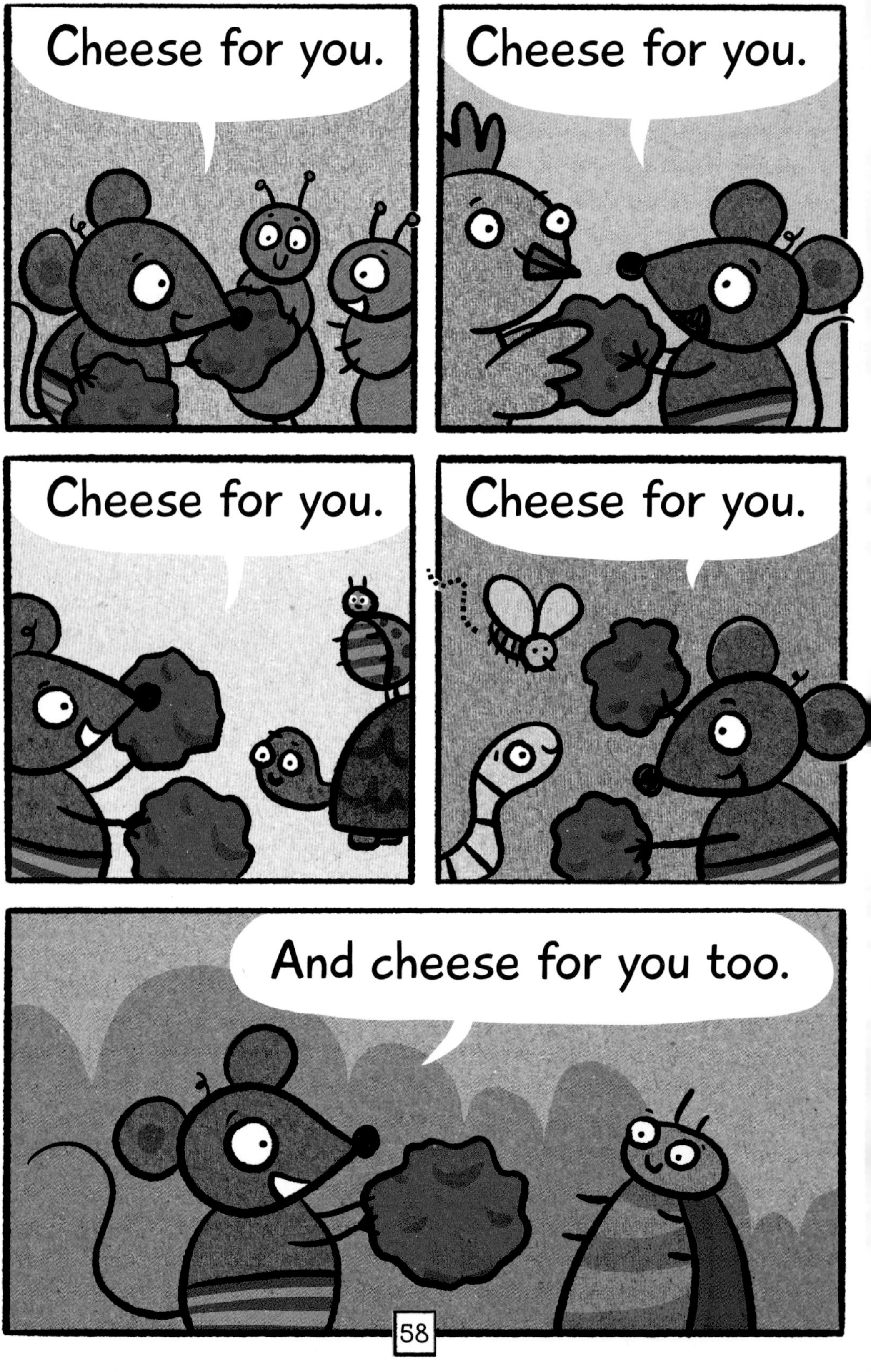
Cheese for you.
Cheese for you.
Cheese for you.
Cheese for you.
And cheese for you too.

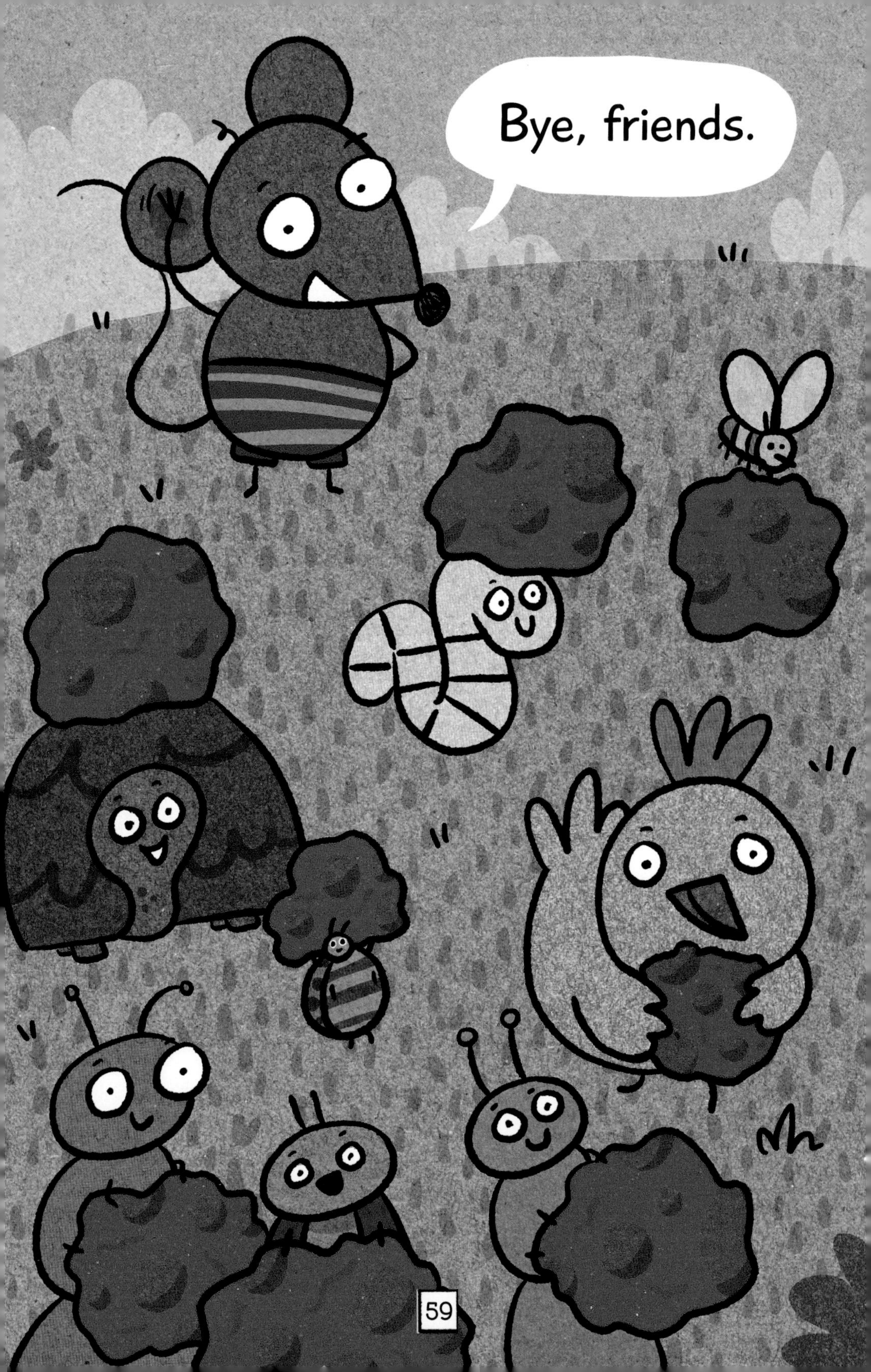
Bye, friends.

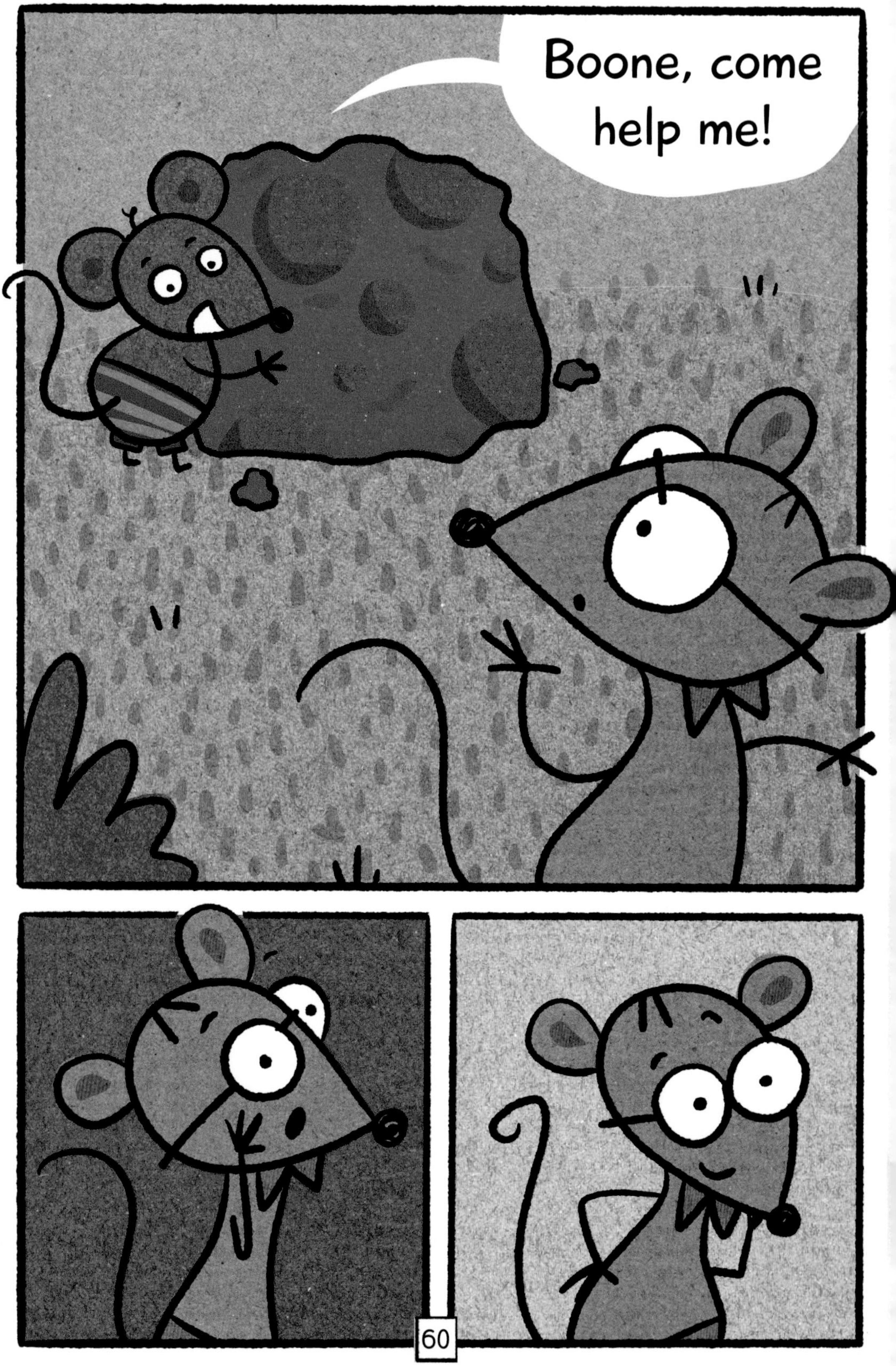
Boone, come help me!

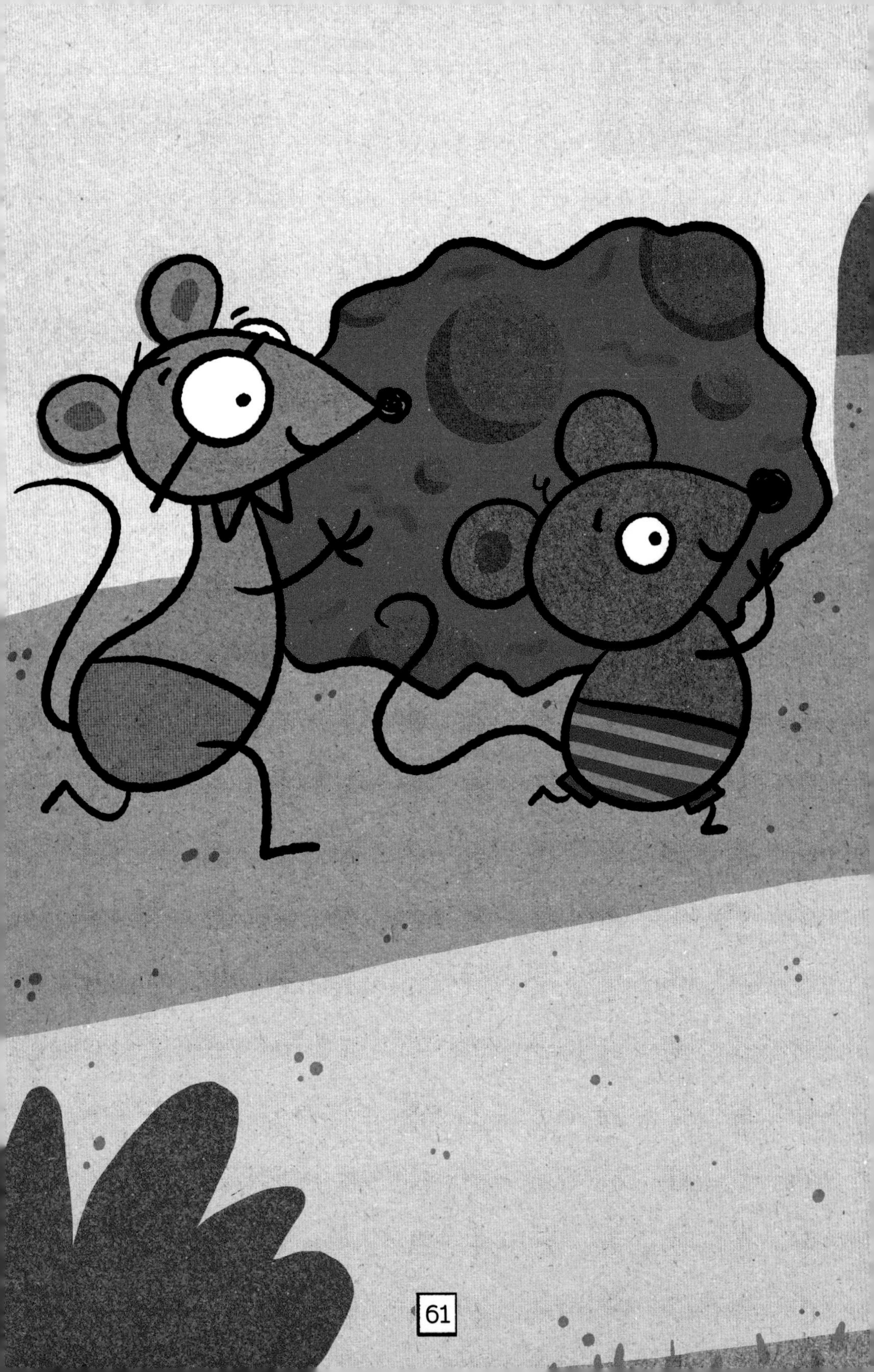

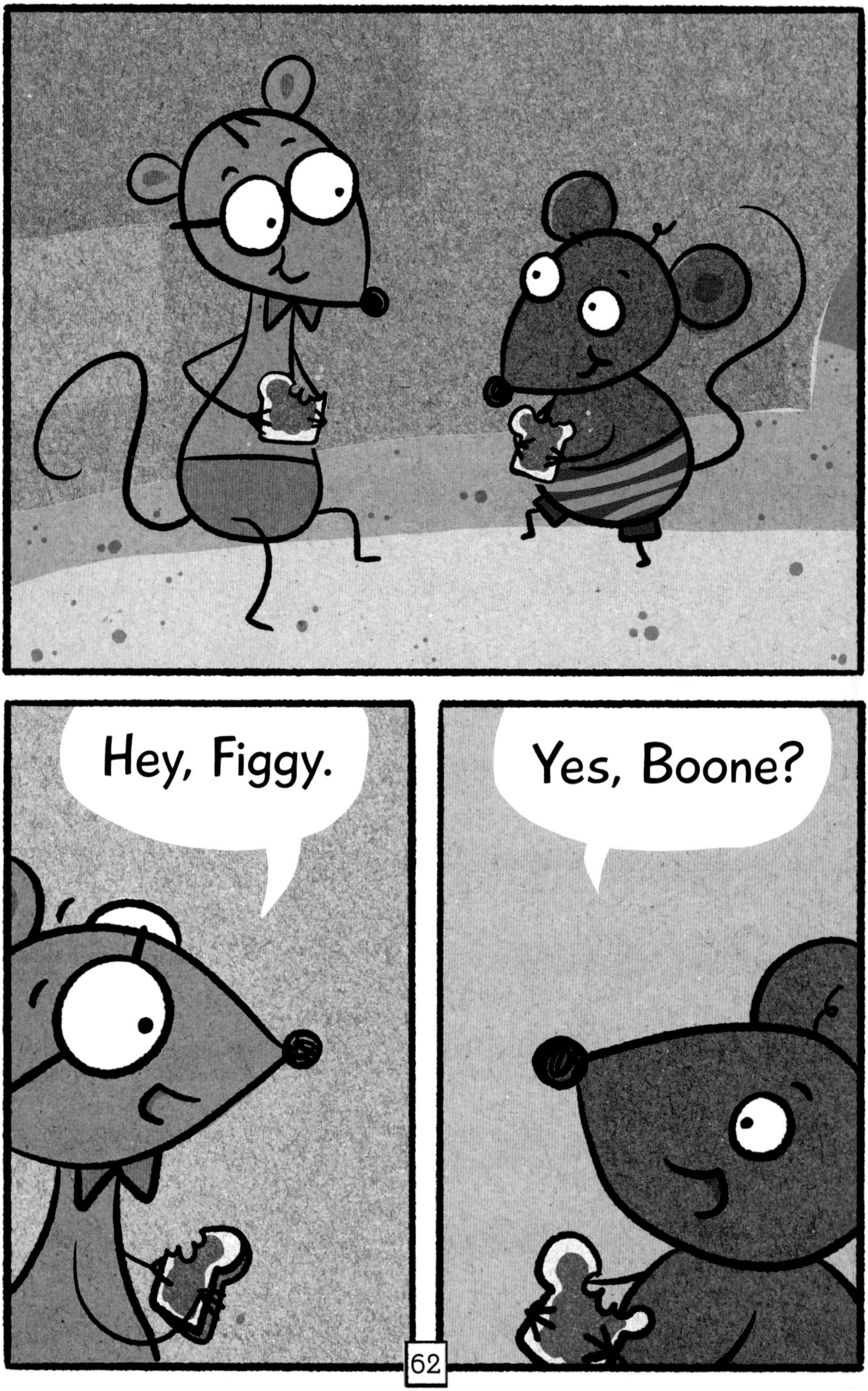
Hey, Figgy.
Yes, Boone?

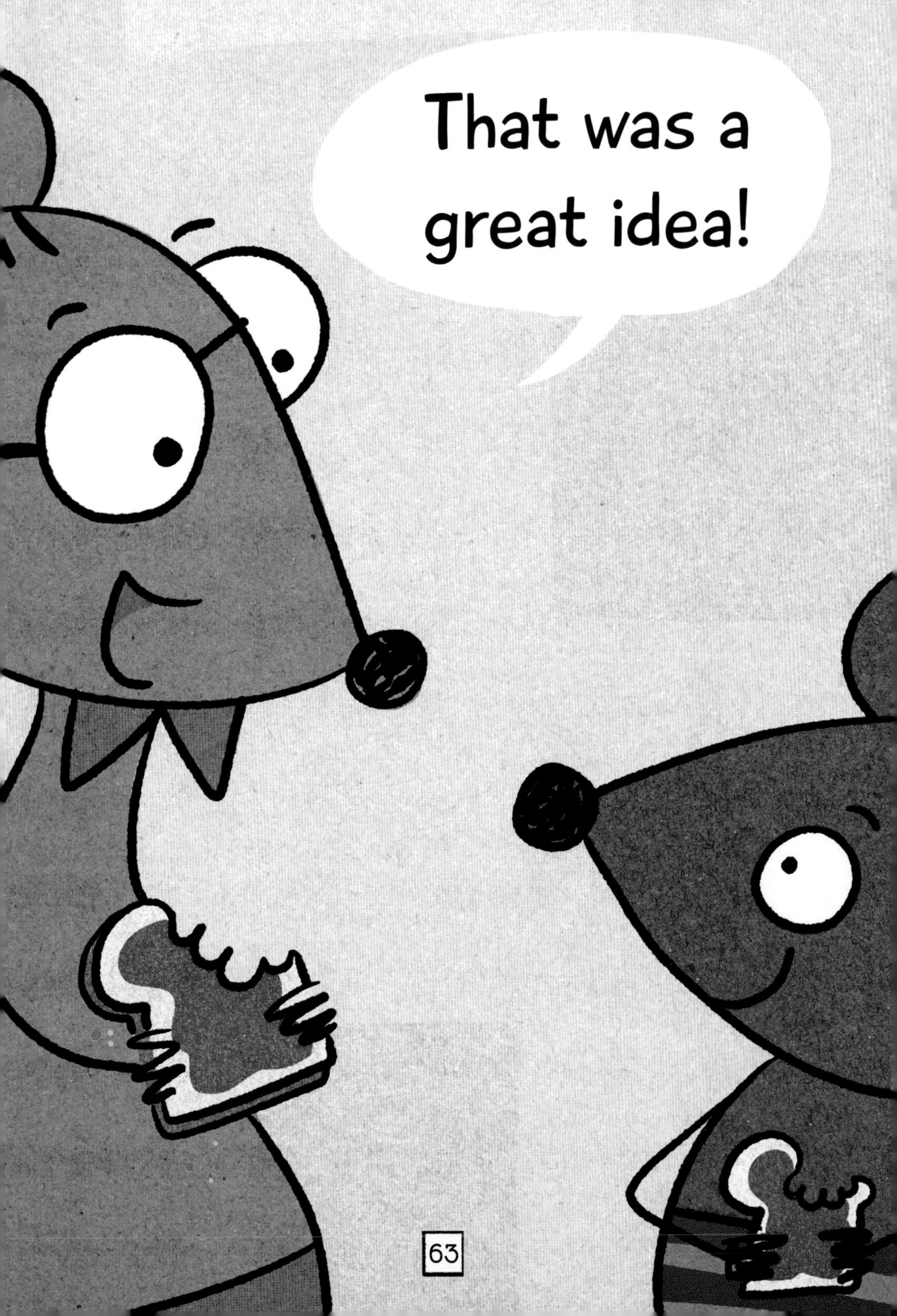
That was a great idea!

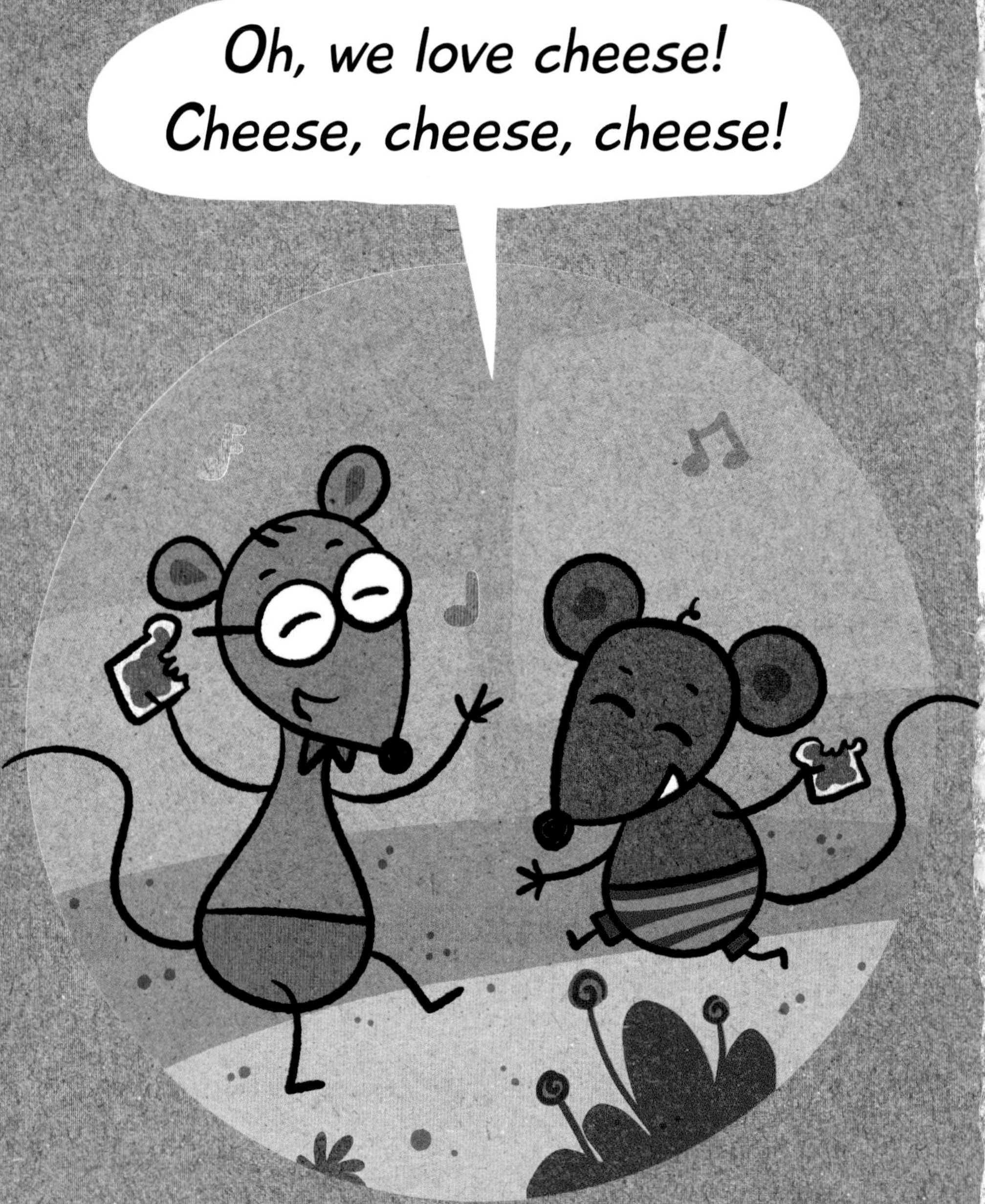
Oh, we love cheese!
Cheese, cheese, cheese!